The Accident

A PORT CITY HIGH NOVEL

S0-AXR-998

SHANNON FREEMAN

SADDLEBACK
EDUCATIONAL PUBLISHING

High School High	*The Accident*
Taken	Listed
Deported	Traumatized
The Public Eye	A Port in Pieces

EDUCATIONAL PUBLISHING
www.sdlback.com

ISBN-13: 978-1-62250-772-6
ISBN-10: 1-62250-772-X
eBook: 978-1-61247-983-5

Printed in Guangzhou, China
NOR/0715/CA21501090

19 18 17 16 15   2 3 4 5 6

ACKNOWLEDGMENTS

First, I want to mention those people who have been here consistently supporting my dream. Carolyn Thibodeaux, Clover Bolden, and all those who are a part of Friends of the Library, you make each book signing special and keep me in mind each time there is an event. For that, I am eternally grateful.

I want to also say thank you to the love of my life, Derrick Freeman. Thank you, God, for giving me the one person who loves me through the good and the bad. Growing with you is better than anything I could have ever imagined.

Thank you to those who are not only

buying my books but diving into the storylines. I love your feedback! A special mention to my sister, Rochelle Jenkins. And thank you to Nadria Nay Nay Turner, Virginia Stidham, Valenta Mathews, Tia Huebel, Felisha Collins, Felise Collins, Shannon Richard, Nakia Crockett, Danielle Infante, Deborah Freeman, Carolyn Warrick, Qiana Brown, Diasheena Gabriel, Evette Rodgers, and the Tiller Family.

There are many parts to me, but the pieces are simply the experiences that I have had the privilege to share with my friends and family. It's funny the stages that we go through and the people we encounter along the way. From PA to Tulsa to Houston to LA and back, you are all a part of me. Together we have lived, laughed, loved, and sometimes even cried. The most important thing, though, was being there for each other. Love you all!

DEDICATION

To Eric Lovilotte, who has touched so many lives in our community, the young and old alike. Gone too soon, forgotten never. We love you.

Prologue

As Marisa, Shane, and Brandi prepared for Marisa's *quinceañera*, they knew that everything had to be perfect. After all, she was about to turn sixteen soon. Normally, that was way too late for a quinceañera, but with all the drama the previous year, all of her quinceañera plans had been put on hold.

When her father was in jail, planning her quinceañera was the last thing she wanted to do. Who would dance with her? Who would lead her transition into adulthood? After all the court costs, who would pay for it? No, she had to wait, and there were only a few more days before she was officially not fifteen anymore. She had to pull this quinceañera off immediately.

In Marisa's culture, the only thing more important than a girl's quinceañera was her wedding. Luckily, Marisa's modeling jobs had helped her family get back on their feet, and now her own money was helping pay for the celebration.

Her family contributed as much as they could. They knew the situation wasn't ideal. No matter how much she protested, her uncles and aunts continued to slip money into her hands whenever they saw her at family gatherings.

"*Tía*, I can't accept your money. You know I'm working now. I can pay for my own quinceañera."

Her mother's sister would hear none of it. "Take it, *mi hija*. A girl does not pay for her own quinceañera. Her family pays for it. We are all doing whatever it takes to give you the celebration you deserve."

"*Muchas gracias*, Auntie."

"*De nada*. Now put that money away. And use it wisely."

Marisa always put the money her family gave for her party into a special savings account. She watched it grow. When she knew she had enough money, she and her mother started planning. With the help of her sisters, everything was in place. It was sure to be the best quinceañera Port City had ever seen.

"I want a quinceañera," Shane said, holding the balloons in place that dangled from the ceiling. They were trying to spell Marisa's name in huge balloon bubble letters, but it was proving to be harder than they had initially thought.

"Your mom's white, your dad's black. That's enough culture for you. Can you let us Hispanics have our own celebration?

Now hold still," Marisa fussed at her. Marisa's nerves were getting to her. She knew there was going to be a large crowd of people. She just wanted everything to be perfect. She worked so hard for this night, and she had looked forward to it for her entire life. The day had finally arrived. She was crossing over into womanhood.

"Hey, y'all!" Brandi shouted, walking into the venue with Young Dub.

"You are *so* late. You said you were going to be here an hour ago," Marisa scolded her best friend. "Why you always on BPT?"

"Don't hate 'cause it takes my choco-late people a little longer than y'all. And you should be thanking me 'cause I swooped up your entertainment for the evening. Who else can get Dub to rap pro bono?"

"Whatever," Marisa responded, turning her attention to Young Dub. "Hey, Dub. Thank you so much for doing this for me."

"Aw, you know I got you, Mari."

She hugged Dub as she walked by. Time to add the finishing touches to the room's décor. She surveyed her work, realizing that her mother and aunts had done almost everything. The bakery had already set up the cake table. The cake was enormous, resembling an extravagant wedding cake, but Marisa's signature colors of black, white, and hot pink gave it a more festive look.

The fruit table was in place, with a chocolate fountain as its centerpiece. There were skewers of pineapple, banana, strawberry, and marshmallow. The gift table was decorated beautifully, but it was still empty. Soon, it would be overflowing with all sorts of luxuries that would assist Marisa's crossover from child to woman. With DJ Dazed set to spin the music and Young Dub performing, this was going to be a bar-raising quinceañera, one that Port City would be talking about for a long time.

She wanted to soak it all in. She knew that after today, this party would be a memory. "Mi hija, you have to get ready!" Her mother's voice snapped her out of the moment. "Everything is beautiful. Now go! Your friends are waiting."

Her mother was right. It was time to get into her first outfit. Her older cousin was there to help her with her hair and makeup. Eva had just turned twenty-one and was possibly the coolest person Marisa had ever met. Being five years older than Marisa, Eva had always been in charge of watching over her when the family had big functions.

She was the best cousin Marisa could ever want. She simply called her *prima*, meaning cousin, and Eva called her the same. They shared a bond, so it was fitting that Eva would be the one to help her on this special day. Eva's own quinceañera had been wonderful. Marisa could only hope her party was just as great.

"I can't believe you'll be sixteen soon, Prima," Eva said to her as she applied mascara to Marisa's eyelashes.

"Right? I wish I could have done this a year ago. I was working to get everything in place, but the trouble with Dad and Romero just ..." Her voice trailed off as if she were thinking about what to say next. "I don't know."

"Hey, today is your day. Don't worry about what happened or didn't happen. You are officially crossing over today. That's all that's important."

"I know. You're right. Thank you so much for being here."

"Where else would I be? It's not every day my little cousin gets presented as a woman in our community."

Marisa thought about what that meant. It was hard to believe.

"Now that should do it. You look beautiful."

Marisa looked like she had stepped

straight out of a page in *LaTeen* magazine. She could hear the music playing
on the other side of the building. That
was the signal indicating the guests were
arriving. The more voices she heard, the
more fluttering butterflies she felt in
her stomach. Her hair and makeup were
finished. It was time to put on her white
dress and veil.

She looked as though she were about
to get married in her beautiful, flowing
gown. She could hear the DJ announcing
her entrance, and she knew it was time.
Her priest was in the reception hall in
order to bless her and the family members
guiding her transition.

After the traditional blessing, the song
"Butterfly Kisses" began to play. She and
her father both loved that song. He took
her hand and danced with her. When the
song was over, Mr. Maldonado removed
her veil and replaced it with a beautiful handcrafted tiara from Mexico. She

looked like a princess as her father spun her around the dance floor.

All of the heartache from the year before dissipated with every spin. It was magic. Tears filled her dad's eyes as he danced with her. When the song ended, he whispered in her ear, "You are my first daughter, the oldest, but you will forever be my baby."

"Oh, Papa," she said, giving him a hug and gently kissing his cheek. For that brief moment, they were the only two people in the room. Hand in hand, he walked her to the back of the building, where she changed into her next outfit. This one was more informal. She could hear the music playing. It was the music of her childhood, traditional and rich.

She knew that meant it was time for her to dance with her cousin Berto. He was the best dancer in their entire family. They had been practicing all summer, and she felt ready. When it was time for her to enter, she ran onto the dance floor confident and beautiful. She started the dance routine immediately. Her solo set the tone for the whole dance.

Berto ran out during the chorus. Everyone knew Berto could dance, but Marisa took everyone by surprise. With every move, she could hear gasps from the audience. As the routine increased in difficulty, her friends and family cheered loudly. She could feel the vibe in the room. Her thin frame defied gravity as she spun around Berto. She ended the routine with an incredible *Dancing with the Stars* move. Both she and Berto were breathing hard and sweating, but they knew they had torn it up.

With the stressful parts of the celebration behind her, Marisa was finally able to focus on her guests. She wanted to kick back and have a good time. Shane and Brandi sat at Marisa's table with her family. Right next to them was a table full of twirlers. It was a perfect party. Everything was just as Marisa had imagined it.

"Girl, I didn't know you could get down like that," Shane told her.

"Right!" Brandi chimed in. "You are going to have to teach me some moves. What did you do, practice all summer?"

"Yeah, I kinda did." Marisa laughed. "When I told you that I was in modeling school, I was secretly practicing with Berto. Oh, and watching every dance show on TV for inspiration."

"You really did great," she heard a male voice say behind her. She could tell by the looks on Brandi and Shane's faces exactly who it was.

Marisa turned quickly to face Trent, who stood regally next to her table. He was the most handsome boy she had ever seen. The contrast of his smooth brown skin and sparkling smile always had an effect on her. "What are you doing here?" she asked in surprise, standing up to hug her boyfriend. He had already left for college in Arkansas, and she knew how difficult it was for him to get back to Texas.

"I couldn't miss your big night," he told her.

"You two knew about this, didn't you?" Marisa asked, turning to her best friends. But they didn't need to respond.

"Now, can your man get a dance?" he asked.

They laughed and had fun just like old times, but they both knew change was coming. They just couldn't say when or what that change would be.

Marisa's thoughts were interrupted by DJ Dazed. She was called to the center of the room. She sat on a chair while guests began to bring specific gifts that symbolized her transition into womanhood.

Her father brought her the traditional doll, dressed like a young princess, which she would keep as a memory of the celebration. Her mother brought her

a scepter, which symbolized her commit-
ment to her community. And her godpar-
ents gave her a small box containing the
prettiest jewelry Marisa had ever seen: a
diamond necklace, a tennis bracelet, and
the earrings to match. She gasped at their
beauty as she looked up at her aunt and
uncle. "Tía, Tío ... it's too much."

"It's from the whole family, mi hija, and
it's for you." Marisa stood from her chair
and hugged them both.

The twirlers presented her with their
own gift. A delicate gold necklace, with
a diamond-encrusted baton charm. "It's
from all of us," Bethany told her.

"It's beautiful," she said with tears
in her eyes. This was even more special
coming from Bethany. The two had grown
close. Bethany wanted to be just like
Marisa. She was in ninth grade and had
never dreamed that the girl she'd heard
so much about in middle school could
be so down-to-earth and real. They made

an immediate connection. And they were inseparable for much of the summer.

She took the microphone and thanked her friends and family. Then DJ Dazed began to do his thing. He was a spinning the latest jams, old-school cuts, and music that would get any celebration cracking. All mixed in together, it made for a great party. The DJ called the men in her family up one by one, and she danced with each of them.

Her little brother, Romero, was the last to join his sister on the dance floor. When they were done dancing, he held her hand tightly. "I'm sorry that you couldn't do this last year. It was my fault." He knew she had been planning her quinceañera when he got himself into all that trouble with gang members from the Fifteens. Everything had changed for his family during that time, and he was still beating himself up over it.

Marisa grabbed her brother's face.

"Look at me, Rom. It's over. Let it go. We all make mistakes. Look around you. This happened just the way it was supposed to. We are all here together. Mom and Dad are legal now. I wouldn't change anything."

He nodded his head. She was his rock. He motioned for his two little sisters, Isi and Nadia, to join them on the dance floor. They danced. They laughed. And they healed. The Maldonados were back.

By the time Young Dub was announced as the guest of honor, Marisa was spent. She sat at the table while her guests crowded Dub on the stage. After he performed two of his hottest songs that had everybody rocking out, he called Marisa onstage. He had written a song just for her. It was the quinceañera song that would go down in history.

Dub had skills, and everybody knew he would put Port City on the map one day. After Young Dub's performance, it was time to relax and enjoy the party. Marisa looked at the people at her table. Shane and Robin, Brandi and Raven, Trent, her sisters and brother, her mom and dad— she was in awe. She scanned the room, watching as her extended family enjoy the evening. At that moment, she felt like the luckiest girl in the world.

CHAPTER 1

Shane

The first day of school at Port City High was uneventful so far for Shane Foster. The back-to-school parties thrown over the weekend seemed childish. She'd seen everybody there was to see and been everywhere there was to go in Port City. During morning break, she watched as the freshman girls bounced around, flirting shamelessly. "Surely it will get better," she said out loud.

"It probably won't, but we have to deal with it," Marisa said, responding to Shane's private thoughts that had slipped out.

"You feeling it too?" Shane asked her.

"No Trent, no Ashton, yeah, I'm feeling it too." They reminisced about the friends they had made the previous school year.

"No Ryan," Shane added sadly. She realized she had really started liking Ryan Petry, last year's editor in chief of the school's newspaper. But she was not willing to let those feelings grow then. She figured it would have made the transition without him even harder. "Trent and Ash made school fun. Now we're left here with the dorks we went to grade school with. Seriously, I'm going to prom alone. I just know I am."

"Hey, hey, hey," Brandi said, brightening up their mood. "Ooh, what's with the long faces, BFFs?"

"We miss our boys," Shane admitted.

"Me too, but they are off in college, the military, or wherever, having a great time. We have to have a great time too. Now perk up. First pep rally today, game tonight, party afterward, and who knows? We could turn this whole year around overnight. Now let's do what we do."

Shane and Marisa both started smiling as they thought about what Brandi was saying. She was right. Those guys weren't thinking about them. They were somewhere having a great time. This was their junior year. There was no time to mourn the past.

"Okay, I'm liking what you're saying. And we'll all be driving soon. You really can't beat that."

"Girl, I can't pass that driver's test fast enough," Brandi told them.

"Hey, that's the bell. Gotta bounce. Thank God I have journalism after lunch. I love going there just to unwind," Shane said. "See y'all later."

Shane had been in Mrs. Monroe's class for three years, and soon she would be running the newspaper. It was only a matter of time before Mrs. Monroe made the big announcement. What better day than today?

The journalism students anxiously filed into Mrs. Monroe's classroom. They knew announcements for new positions on the newspaper and the yearbook would be happening soon. Everyone in that room had worked hard last year to meet Ryan Petry's expectations. He had run a tight ship. The new editor in chief had big shoes to fill.

It usually took a minute or two to get the class to settle down. But today, the students hung on Mrs. Monroe's every word, not wanting to miss anything.

"Well, good afternoon, class," she said, feeling the tension in the room. "I see that y'all are ready for some announcements, huh?"

"Come on, Mrs. Monroe. You're killing us," one of the seniors blurted out.

"I'm pleased to say that I have chosen

some really great people to run the paper this year. I had some hard decisions to make, but I hope you will respect my choices."

Mrs. Monroe continued to talk to the class, but Shane had stopped listening. She hoped she was not one of those hard decisions. Surely she had gotten the editor in chief position. Journalism was all she had. It was the only thing she could be sure about in her life.

"Your new editor in chief for this school year is Whitley Harris," Mrs. Monroe said. Shane gasped. She felt like all the air had left her body. She needed fresh air, water, something. She had to pull it together. Whitley stood up and gave her thanks to the team. But Shane didn't listen to a word of it. She was disappointed. She was angry.

Mrs. Monroe started to speak again, something about a new position, something about the paper growing this year, something about ... "Shane Foster, our new managing editor. She will work closely with Whitley. The two-woman team is just what we need this year. I'm confident they will both do a great job. Shane, would you like to say something?"

She didn't know what to say. She couldn't come across as ungrateful. "I look forward to working with each of you. It'll be a great school year." There! Short and sweet. She could see that the class looked to her as an advisor. Someone they should respect. But she was having trouble with this one, and she knew there was one person who wasn't fooled: Mrs. Monroe.

Once all jobs had been divided, Mrs. Monroe asked to speak with Shane. "You okay with your new position?" she whispered, sensing that Shane wasn't happy.

"I'm fine."

"I would have given it to you, but Whitley worked so hard last year. I have to reward that. It's her last year and she's ready. Please try to understand."

"It's okay, Mrs. Monroe. I get it." Shane gave her a tight smile. The bell rang, signaling students could go to their next class. Shane was so relieved. She didn't want to be mad at Mrs. Monroe, but she was. She knew she would have to find some way to deal with it.

CHAPTER 2

Marisa

As Marisa turned the corner to enter the lunchroom, she spotted a freshman closing the locker that used to belong to her boyfriend, Trent, only months ago. How many times had she stood at that locker, waiting for him to meet her? And now this little kid was shoving his backpack there before going into the lunchroom. He had no idea the memories that had been made near that very piece of school property. He had no idea that Ashton, Trent's best friend, had the locker right next to his. Even if he found out, he probably wouldn't care. Those were her memories, not his.

She was deep in thought about Trent when two girls, who looked like they could have passed for ten-year-olds, stopped her in her tracks.

"Um, are you Marisa Maldonado?" a cute little Hispanic girl with pretty brown eyes asked nervously. Her friend was an African American girl with lots of swag and an adorable, round face. They looked hopeful. Was this the right girl?

"Um, yeah, why?" she asked, a little aggravated that they had interrupted her Trent moment.

Each girl had a magazine clutched in her hand. They both looked so young. It made Marisa mad at herself for snapping at them. They reminded her of her besties minus two years.

"I'm Bella, and this is Danaya," she said, introducing her friend. "We are huge fans of yours."

"Of mine?" Marisa asked, confused. "You must have the wrong person."

"You're so funny," Danaya giggled.

"We don't have too many models in Port City," Bella added. "Do you know how many Hispanic girls are looking up to you? I'm just one of many."

"Well, I'm not even Hispanic," Danaya said, "but I think your modeling is awesome. I would love to be a model one day. Do you mind signing our copies of your Gap ad?"

"We saw that report they did about you on the news ..."

" ... and we vowed we would find you on the first day of school so we could get your autograph."

Marisa took the magazines from their hands. She used the empty hall monitor's desk as a support to sign her very first autographs. The moment was surreal. Both girls were still chattering on and on about how they wanted to walk in her footsteps one day. And about her being an inspiration to other girls in Port City.

"Do you think maybe we could have lunch with you one day?" Danaya asked her, full of hope.

"Sure," Marisa answered, still feeling a bit awkward about the encounter.

Both of the girls looked excited about the idea of having lunch with her. Marisa didn't know what to say to them anymore. She looked for a quick escape. The whole thing was just weird. She spotted Brandi coming down the hallway and waved her over. "Excuse me, ladies. My lunch date just arrived. Hey, B!" she said, turning her attention.

"O-M-G, what is it like being friends with a supermodel?" Danaya asked Brandi.

"Huh, who?" Brandi asked, confused. "Oh, Marisa," she responded, finally understanding who they meant. She giggled a little when she looked at Marisa, who was obviously uncomfortable. "It's very glamorous," she said, making her friend squirm. "It's like having your very own rock star. I scream every time she walks in the room, and I roll out a red carpet when she stays the night at my house."

The girls hung on Brandi's every word until she was jerked away by Marisa. "Okay, that's enough. Nice meeting you both," Marisa said, pushing Brandi through the lunchroom doors. "That was not funny," she hissed.

"Girl, yes it was. Don't be embarrassed 'cause you have fans. You know I'm your number one fan and cheerleader."

"What'd I miss?" Shane asked, joining her friends.

"Nothing," Marisa said defensively.

"Marisa's embarrassed because she's famous with the ninth graders. They got her autograph and everything."

"That is nothing to be embarrassed about. Are you crazy? You had to know this was coming. Look how many followers you have on Friender. Everybody in Port City wants to know who you are. It's huge being a model from a little town like this," Shane said, trying to convince her friend.

"I guess, but you know I like my little group and no more," Marisa replied. "I'm not a social butterfly like the two of you."

As they sat down at a table, they were greeted by Mrs. Montgomery, Port City High School's principal. She always seemed to know what was going on. Did she bug their phones or something?

"Good afternoon, ladies."

"Good afternoon, Mrs. Montgomery," they said.

"Marisa, I just wanted to stop by and ask if it would be okay if we have a small reception in your honor. Some of the younger girls have really shown an interest in you and your work. I thought it'd be a great idea to have a meet and greet. Would you be interested?" she asked.

"Um ... honestly, Mrs. Montgomery—" she started to say.

"She would love to," Shane volunteered.

"And we will help with the ceremony if you need us," Brandi added.

"I will have my secretary start working on it immediately. Thank you so much. The girls around here could use a little guidance. Excuse me," Mrs. Montgomery said as she walked away.

"I'm not guidance. They are trying to turn me into the Port City Hannah Montana. Well, the throwback Hannah Montana, before she got all fast. This ain't cool."

"Girl, it is *so* cool," Shane said, sliding into the chair next to her and looping her arm through her best friend's arm.

"It is *very* cool," Brandi said with a huge smile.

Marisa started to see things through their eyes. She hadn't wanted to be in the limelight. She just wanted to pursue her passion, but her passion had put her here. She couldn't let Port City down.

"Okay, okay," she said. "I guess it is a *little* cool." Her mood quickly changed when she thought about sharing this moment with Trent. She had started on this modeling path with Trent by her side. After all, he was the one who brought her to that first open call and encouraged her ambition. His support gave her the confidence to win that Gap ad. Now, he was far away in Arkansas.

They had barely talked since he left. He rarely answered his phone. And when he did, he always had to rush off. It was making her uneasy about their relationship. She desperately wanted to text him and tell him about her day, but she didn't want to set herself up to be rejected.

"What's wrong?" Shane asked, noticing her mood change.

"Nothing," she said as a tear formed in her eye. "I'm fine."

She didn't want to complain to her friends. It wasn't going to change anything. Marisa was determined to embrace her new life. The old one seemed to be fading away.

CHAPTER 3

Brandi

"Mom, I'm home!" Brandi yelled out as she walked into the house after her first day of school.

Her sister came running down the stairs to greet her. "Hey, B! I had such a good time at school today. Being a fifth grader is the best. And guess what?" Raven never stopped to take a breath. She just kept going. "We are going to go on five field trips this year. I can't wait."

"That sounds so wonderful, RaRa. Where's Mom? Have you seen her?"

Their dad joined them downstairs.

"She ran to the store to get something that she forgot for the shrimp scampi," he said. "How was your day, baby girl?" he asked Brandi, kissing her on the forehead.

"It was pretty cool. You are looking at the new co-captain of the varsity cheerleading squad. I really can't believe it. I never thought I would be co-captain. My hard work this summer really did pay off."

"Why didn't you think you would be chosen?" her dad asked.

"Like maybe I wasn't good enough. Like Coach didn't think I was good enough."

"Yeah, well, I went to high school with your coach, Miss Michaels. We never really saw eye to eye growing up. Maybe she held that against you up to now. Maybe she thought you were like your old dad. Now, after two years she knows your personality and your skills, so she is finally rewarding you with what you deserve."

"I suppose that could be," replied Brandi.

"The important thing is you earned your spot on the squad, and nobody can take it away from you."

It felt good for her dad to be on her side. It felt good to have a father to talk to about things like making co-captain. Raven stood quietly, listening to their exchange. They both basked in the moment of having a real dad.

"Honeys! I'm home!" announced Catherine Haywood. She came into the kitchen through the garage. Everyone rushed to help.

"Hey, let me help you with those," Brandi's dad said as he relieved her mom of some grocery bags.

"Thanks, honey. Hey, my girls, how was school?" she asked both kids, kissing them enthusiastically on the cheek.

How their lives had changed. Her dad was now a recovering drug addict. His addiction had caused a rift in their family. During that time, her parents were constantly fighting, and her mother was working to replace the money he squandered away. It had been part of the reason Brandi had fallen for a guy on the Internet who turned out to be a crazed kidnapper. She had gone through a lot, but after two months, she had been rescued.

Now that her father was back from rehab, Brandi and Raven had both of their parents' loving support. It was amazing.

They were a close-knit family once again, and the girls were enjoying every minute. Brandi loved her mother and father. Their family had truly gone through a rough patch, but things were definitely looking up.

Around school there were flyers everywhere promoting the Young Dub concert that was being held at the Port City Civic Center. Brandi was shocked that Dub hadn't told her he was performing. They had met at the beginning of summer. To

Brandi's surprise, Catherine Haywood worked with Dub's auntie. And Brandi insisted that she get an introduction to the hot Texas rapper. The two immediately clicked.

They weren't a couple or anything, but they were close enough for her to know about the concert. She needed backstage passes for her and her girls, and he hadn't even reached out. She knew she was going to have to contact him before the concert.

When her girls met at their lockers after school on Friday, each held their own copy of the flyer.

"I can't believe Dub is trying to diss," Shane said, upset that she was finding out about the concert from a flyer. "He's treating us like he don't cut for our crew. B, you need to check yo boy."

"He could have mentioned it at my super sweet quinceañera."

"Do you *have* to say 'my super sweet

quinceañera' every time?" Shane questioned Marisa.

"Hey, I like saying it," Marisa retorted with a smile. "Who else can say that? I had both a quinceañera and a sweet sixteen, hence my ..."

"Yeah, yeah, like I was saying, B, holler at Dub, or else we are gonna have to go to the studio."

"You ain't said nothing but a word. Let's go to the studio. I'm so down," Brandi announced.

"We don't even have a ride to the studio, and I'm not trying to find anybody to take us," Marisa said.

"Who doesn't have a ride?" Shane asked, shaking a set of car keys at her friends and smiling mischievously.

"You little sneak," Marisa said, snatching the keys from her hand. "Let's ride. I got shotgun!"

They blasted their music as soon as the car was on. Windows down, music up,

Friday afternoon had never felt so good. The freedom of Shane driving made them all feel a little more grown up, even though Marisa and Brandi weren't behind the wheel of the car.

"I can't believe that Robin let you take her car to school!" Brandi yelled over the music. Shane's older sister never let her drive her car since Shane didn't have a license. Now that Robin and Gavin had a son, they were way too serious for Shane's liking. There was a time before they had Aiden they would have probably thrown her the keys. No driver's license? Whatever.

Shane immediately turned the music down. "Okay, confession ... she didn't let me. I just kind of took it. She's out of town with Gavin and Aiden. Mom and Dad weren't there, so ..."

"So you're going to get your butt kicked later on today," Brandi said.

"It'll be so worth it, though," Marisa squealed. "This is freakin' awesome."

When they arrived at the studio, Young Dub was already in the booth. His producer, Beaty B, was on the boards, giving him direction. "Dub, give me more on that last verse. They gotta feel you on that, man."

"Beaty, roll it back," Dub told him. He began to rap over a beat that the girls had never heard. It was soulful. The beat itself was the background music to Dub's life. He began to tell his story, not a made-up industry story, his *real* story. The girls looked at each other as they witnessed Texas rap history being made. This song would put Dub on the map. It was that powerful.

When he came out of the booth, he went straight to Brandi, who was laughing with Beaty B. Shane was propped up on Beaty's lap. All three of the girls loved Beaty. He was just a laid-back guy who seemed to never have a bad day. Dub was cool, but Beaty was a big teddy bear.

When Dub walked into the room, all of the attention turned to him. He tried to kiss Brandi on the forehead, but she wasn't in the mood to accept a kiss from him.

"What? You walk in my session to dog me out?"

"No, you dogged me out. I came here to get that straight."

"Do we need to talk in private?" he asked, noticing the menacing looks from the girls.

"No, you know that we are like family up in here. You know why I'm mad, Dub." Marisa cleared her throat and Shane followed suit. "I'm sorry, why *we* are mad."

"Man, girls be trippin', for real," Dub said, getting annoyed. Beaty B started laughing; they weren't mad at him. This was Dub's problem. "Talk to me, woman. I have to get back to work."

"What's up with the concert? How come I gotta find out from some flyer? No backstage passes? Nothing?"

"Look, I'm going to stop you right there, 'cause yo neck rolling is too much for me. *I* just found out about the concert. The Port City Youth Council called and asked if I was free. They took care of the rest. Beaty, hit them with those platinum passes we had made for the staff. Now get out the studio with your bad vibes."

"You know I love you, right?" Brandi asked, giving Dub a kiss on the lips.

"Uh-huh. That won't last past Sunday. I know you, B. Hit yo boy later."

CHAPTER 4

The Concert

Marisa, Shane, and Brandi worked feverishly to get their outfits just right for the concert. Every detail was in place. After all, they set the precedent at the school for swag, and they could not be upstaged, not tonight. They had backstage passes to the biggest concert that Port City had seen in a long time. Young Dub might be a home-town rapper, but it wasn't every day that he did a concert at the civic center. This was special.

"My butt looks so big in these shorts,"

Brandi said, looking at her backside in Shane's full-length mirror.

"It's not the shorts," Marisa said dryly. "It always looks like that no matter what you have on."

"That butt is just big, period. Home-grown from the Port City soil is what that is," Shane laughed, joining Marisa.

"Y'all are mean," Brandi said, eyeing the distressed denim shorts that she paired with a red chiffon shirt and her leopard print heels. Her makeup set her outfit off. She found a red lipstick that was the exact same color as her shirt. "I like my butt. I got it from my mama," she said, dancing and dropping it to the floor.

"Girl, if I could do that, you couldn't talk to me," Shane said. She had gotten her mama's rhythm and she knew it. Her skin was caramel, but she was white on the inside. It showed when she tried to dance. She gave herself a once-over in the bath-room mirror. Her hair was laid as usual.

She wore a simple black skirt with a loose-fitting tank that read, I Know. It showed off her flat stomach and draped down past her waist in the back. It was business in the back, but party in the front.

Shane paired her outfit with her snake-skin pumps and silver bangles. "Simple and cute," she said, kissing her reflection. "I can't wait to get to the concert. I wish I could bring my camera, but I can't risk anything happening to it," she said. "Oh, Mari," she exclaimed, "I love that dress!"

"Thanks," Marisa said in her quiet way. She knew it was beautiful. It was one of the things that she had bought at the Galleria in Houston after a photo shoot. The khaki dress had stratcgically placed gold sequins woven into the material that complimented her model's frame. There was no overkill on the sequins like on some dresses. That would have cheapened her look. Marisa looked expensive and put together. The gold strappy heels she paired with her dress complemented it perfectly.

Brandi began screaming while reading a text on her cell phone.

"Is everything okay in here?" Mrs. Foster asked, opening the door to Shane's bedroom.

"I'm so sorry, Mrs. Foster. I just got a text that has me all excited. Dub is sending his limo to pick us up for the concert." She started to scream again. Shane and Marisa joined her.

"That's so awesome!" Shane exclaimed.

"Not really," said Mrs. Foster. "After all Brandi has been through? There's no way you are getting into a strange limo without supervision. I'm following you in the car."

"Mom, we are in the eleventh grade, and we will all be together. It's okay."

"Well, I'm calling Cat and Lupe to get permission first. If they say it's okay with them, then it's okay." She left the room to call the girls' mothers.

Shane grabbed her camera and set it on her tripod. "We have to remember this night." They posed as the automatic timer snapped their pictures. When they were done, her mom came back with permission for them to ride in the limo. They were under strict orders to keep in touch throughout the night. With all the plans in place, the girls were excited for the evening to begin.

The doorbell rang and an older man dressed in a chauffeur's uniform greeted Mrs. Foster.

"Ma'am, can you please inform Brandi Haywood that her ride is here?"

"Girls, your ride is here!" she yelled for them to come down. "Make sure you take care of my girls," she said as she slipped twenty dollars into the driver's hand.

All three of them thoroughly enjoyed the limo ride. Third Coast Records music was loaded into the sound system, so they partied all the way to the concert with sparkling water in their champagne flutes.

"Girl, Dub is pulling out his best game on you. You better be careful," Shane said, laughing as they waited for the driver to open their door.

As each of them stepped out, the crowd waiting to get into the concert began to notice them. They could hear their names being whispered. They were the topic of conversation.

"Did they just get out of a limo?"

"Is that the girl who's a model?"

"That was Shane Foster."

"That's the girl who was abducted for, like, two months, remember? What's her name? Brandi?"

They were whisked past the crowd, then led to a side door with the passes they had gotten from Dub. No waiting in lines, no pushing and shoving, no money to get in ... sweet.

"I can't believe we come here all the time. This is the same place they have company picnics, and the same place where they have the gumbo cook off. Walking down that path has never felt like this before," Marisa exclaimed.

"I can get used to VIP treatment," Brandi said, smiling.

When they arrived inside the concert hall, they were escorted to Dub's dressing room. They were told they could wait there until the concert started. As they sat in the small, cramped dressing area, the magic of their arrival faded quickly. As time moved on, there was no sign of Dub or Beaty. They saw their outfits wasting away right before their eyes.

"I'm bored. Let's get outta here," Shane told them.

They walked out of the dressing room and wound up backstage as the engineers and sound people moved around, trying to get everything perfect for the first artist coming onstage. The music that vibrated to keep the crowd happy was definitely throwback. The DJ was tearing it up, and the crowd was loving it. If nothing else, they were ready for a show.

As they peeked out at the audience, they saw how massive the crowd was. The whole civic center was packed, and everyone was partying and getting geared up for the artists to come onstage. One thing about Third Coast Music, art truly imitated life. It was fresh, popping, fun, and real.

"Ladies and gentlemen, may I have your attention, please. We are going to party tonight and enjoy some good music. No fighting, no disrespecting, just straight up fun. Everybody ready to blow the roof off this piece tonight? Our first artist needs no introduction. Port City's own Lil Flo!"

"I need to feel the crowd's vibe. I can't stay backstage. I'll meet up with y'all in a sec," Shane told them, but they weren't listening to her. They were right behind her, carefully walking down the stairs along the side of the stage and squeezing into the crowd.

And that's how the concert kicked off. Lil Flo sure could write music. It was the type of stuff that all females had jamming as they rolled the strip, the seawall, or just kicked it with their girls. That girl was plain real.

"*Tell yo dude, I ain't tryna be rude. Stop callin', stop tweetin', stop textin' me too. Lil Flo been known as a Baby G ...*" Her rhymes went hard, and the beats were bangin'. The girls were all rapping with her as loud as they could.

The vibe was hot for Dub when he came onstage. "We love you, Dub!" the audience screamed.

"I love you too, mami," he said in a way that would melt ice.

He started with songs everybody

knew. You could barely hear Dub as the crowd rapped along with him.

"Y'all like that one, huh?" he asked everyone in between songs. "Well, I have a new one I hope you like just as much. I may need a little assistance with this one, though," he said, searching the crowd for the perfect girl. But he knew exactly who he was looking for.

"Do you mind helping me out?" he asked Brandi as the spotlight found her in the crowd. She climbed the staircase, holding his hand. It felt like a dream, and she never wanted to wake up.

The song was awesome. When he got to the chorus, he got on one knee and held her hand. "*When you ain't right, I ain't right. When you gotta fight, mami, we both gotta fight. I know it's been rough, but you been through enough. So after tonight, I'll be your knight.*"

Brandi held back a tear. He had written that song for her. She knew he had. It was her life. It had been rough, and it felt like Dub just got it.

When the concert was over, the girls were pumped. They knew they had their parents' permission to stay out very late, as long as they stayed in touch. Luckily, there was an after-party at Dub's hotel room to keep the fun going.

"I'm ready to get out of here," Marisa said as they waited by the limo.

"Marisa!" she heard someone yelling her name. "Mari!" The girl waved frantically from the entrance.

"Who is that waving like a crazy person?" Shane asked Marisa.

Marisa couldn't make out the girl until she started walking toward them. "That's Bethany. She's my baby girl."

By the time Bethany made it to them, she was out of breath. "I saw you by the limo and didn't want to intrude."

"So you yell her name across a parking—" Brandi asked her.

"It's okay," Marisa said, cutting Brandi off. "If anybody can embarrass the mess out of me after a concert and get away with it, it would be you."

"I'm sorry," she said, bringing her voice down to a whisper. "Did I embarrass you?"

"Okay, you're right. She is lovable, but she's rough around the edges," Shane said, laughing at Marisa's young protégé.

"Look at all those li'l groupies hanging out by the door, looking thirsty. They better leave my man alone," Brandi said, giving all sorts of attitude.

Shane and Marisa looked at each other suspiciously.

"Your man?" Marisa asked first.

"Oh my goodness, that song really was for you," Bethany said naively.

"I thought y'all were just friends," Shane told her. "And you're supposed to be on a break from dating, 'member?"

"I know, but he's just so sweet. I mean,

you were all there tonight. You would have both given in by now too."

"Girl, last week," Shane said, laughing. "Dub!" Shane hollered, making all the other girls turn and look toward them. He waved at her thankfully and dismissed his fans. He didn't want to linger at the door, and Shane gave him a good excuse.

"You ladies ready for the real party?" he asked, joining them next to the limo.

"We were born ready," Shane told him.

"Hey, y'all have fun! Call me, Mari," Bethany told her as she walked away.

Bethany was halfway through the parking lot when the limo cut her off. The back window slowly crept down. "Hey, mami, we can't have you waiting out here alone. Come to the after-party," Dub said with a smile that could get anybody to do anything. He truly was a charmer.

"Me? I can come too? Really?"

"Girl, get in the doggone limo already,"

Brandi said. Bethany was a breath of fresh air for them. They were all immune to the newness of being in high school, but her eyes still lit up. They missed being innocent.

As soon as everyone was situated, Dub grabbed Brandi and pulled her next to him.

"Aw, you two are so cute," Marisa said. Watching the budding romance made her miss Trent even more. She took out her phone, about to text him some love, but she decided against it. She had already reached out many times, and he wasn't reciprocating. She had to be strong enough not to call or text again. She was not going to chase him.

When they got to the hotel, the party was already in full swing. All of Dub's friends were there, partying before Dub even left the civic center. Girls in skimpy swimsuits were running around, jumping in and out of the hot tub.

"Hey, there are swimsuits hanging in the closet if y'all want to change. I'm gonna get mine right after I catch up with my boys. I'll meet you back by the Jacuzzi."

The remainder of the night was filled with friends, fun, and late-night Waffle House brought straight to the hotel by one of Dub's boys. With all of the girls there, Brandi was sure Dub wouldn't pay her much attention, but she was wrong. He only had eyes for her the entire night.

If they thought she had been won over before, they were sure of it by two o'clock in the morning. The limo pulled up to Shane's, and it was obvious that Dub had won his woman, hands down.

"What a wonderful night," Shane said as she unlocked the door.

"I had so much fun," Brandi added.

"It was amazing!" Bethany gushed. She had permission from her mom to stay with Marisa. Her mom had fallen in love with Marisa too. They thought that her life was picture-perfect. They had no idea she was hurting on the inside. The thought of Trent could bring her to tears at any given moment. It was hard, and she was going through it all alone. The last thing she wanted to do was bring her girls down with her or disappoint Bethany.

"Yeah, great night." She forced herself to smile, but inside, her mind was on Trent. *I wonder who is making him smile tonight.*

CHAPTER 5

Marisa

$\mathcal{I}$t was a hot and humid morning when Marisa and her mother began the long ride to Houston. It had been nearly six months since the Gap audition totally changed her life. What started out so fun, now felt like hard work. Marisa wasn't excited about anything anymore. With her relationship problems on her mind, she wasn't the same person. She was trying to be, but nothing felt quite the same.

"Mi hija, you can stop modeling now. Papa's business is doing much better. You don't have to do this if you don't want to," her mother told her as they rode the familiar I-10 path to Houston.

"Mama, why do you say that? I love modeling."

"You do? It looks like this is starting to take a toll. Is anything else bothering you?" she asked suspiciously, like a mother would.

"No, I'm fine. I'm just tired today." She wasn't ready to go into detail with her mother, or anybody besides Trent for that matter. She had to digest what was happening to her relationship and the effect it was having on her. She needed to get closure on this situation, and she needed to do it quickly.

When she arrived on set, there were a dozen white roses at her makeup table. The card read, "Happy Birthday, from Miller & Miller Modeling." It made her smile. She knew Marcie Miller had taken a chance on her. Even though Marisa had the looks and the talent, she knew having someone represent her and invest time in her was huge. She and Marcie had a growing relationship. She was definitely someone Marisa liked and respected. She could see herself as an agent one day, helping young hopeful models.

Marcie had shared her story with her. She started out just like Marisa, modeling at a very young age. She transformed her modeling career into the agency that she owned.

The roses had given Marisa the boost she needed to make it through the photo shoot. It was the first time anyone had ever given her roses as a gift, and it made her feel special.

When the camera started shooting, she let go of the stress. She was in the moment and giving the shoot exactly what it needed. The photographer was impressed. He showed her the pictures as he praised her work. She couldn't help but be proud of herself.

"You did great today." Her mother smiled, giving her a big hug.

"Thanks, Mama. It felt really good. I'm so thankful." Her confidence was through the roof. She wanted to call Trent. It felt right. "Will you give me a minute to make a phone call while I gather my things?"

"Sure, baby. I'll take your flowers and meet you at the car."

She dialed Trent's cell phone, but there was no answer. She decided to try his dorm room. His roommate would answer sometimes. "Hello?" an unfamiliar voice answered the phone.

"I'm sorry. I must have the wrong number," Marisa responded. "I was looking for Trent, Trent Walker."

"Bay! Somebody's on the phone for you!" the girl yelled. There was a long pause. "He wants to know who it is."

Marisa was stunned. She felt like she had been hit by a ton of bricks. *Who is this girl? Why did she call him bay? Is she the reason he has been avoiding me?* She could feel the tears welling up. Her stomach began to do flip-flops, and she knew she had to get out of the building. She needed some air.

"Hello? Are you still there? Who is this?" the girl on the phone asked.

"You did great today at the shoot, really great. I can't wait to work with you again," the photographer said, interrupting the call. "Are you okay?"

Her face was pale. The girl on the phone was still asking her questions. The photographer was talking nonstop. Marisa just wanted to run. "I'm fine. I had a great day too. Thank you so much. Sorry I have to run. My mom's waiting downstairs. Thanks again." She had to remain professional no matter what was going on in her private life. She gathered her belongings and quickly walked away.

"Are you talking to me?" the girl asked her, getting more and more annoyed.

"No, I'm not talking to you. Just tell Trent to call his *ex-girlfriend* when he gets a second. 'K?" She hung up the phone and hurried to the car. As soon as she was sitting in the passenger's seat of her mom's car, she broke down.

"Baby, what's the matter?" her mother asked. Marisa couldn't respond. She felt as though she was going to vomit.

"I can't, Mama. I can't ... please, just drive. Let's get outta here." She cried herself to sleep and woke up when she got home to cry some more.

Normally, her mother would bring her to school when they got back into town from a shoot, but she seemed to know her daughter needed some alone time. Marisa went straight to her room and didn't come out for the entire night.

CHAPTER 6

Shane

As the days dragged on, Shane's disdain for school grew. Boredom and monotony set in. *There's nothing exciting about being here.* She stood in front of the office door, trying to get to the other side of the hallway. Students crowded the way, making her path to class virtually impossible.

"Come on, let's get to class!" the principal shouted on her bullhorn.

The mad rush of students frantically trying to avoid detention forced Shane to fly forward, hit another student, and drop the books she was carrying. "Great," she said, disgusted.

"Let me help you with that," a man said, bending down to pick up the books before other students trampled them. He quickly gathered her belongings and stood up. "Here you go," he said, looking directly at Shane for the first time. He took her breath away. He was *that* guy, the one who could make you go weak in the knees the first time you looked at him. Butterflies danced in her stomach. Shane Foster was at a loss for words.

"You're welcome ... I mean, thanks," she said. She gave him a genuine smile.

"Coach, get these kids moving to class. We need to clear the hall."

"Yes, ma'am," he responded. "You better be getting to class now. Don't be late," he warned Shane.

"Oh, right. Headed there now." She walked away from him and quickly threw her books in her locker. She looked back to see if he was still standing there. He politely waved at her and walked down the hall to return to his own classroom.

He's a teacher? Really? He doesn't look like any teacher I've ever seen before.

She was sitting in math class, but she was thinking about the man she had just bumped into. She didn't even know his name. Coach? That's what the principal had called him.

She was in la-la land, dreaming about his smooth caramel-colored skin that was only a few shades darker than her own, his strong cheekbones, the muscles she saw bulging from his shirt ...

"Shane, I asked you a question," she heard her teacher say.

"Huh, what? Sorry, Mister Mutomba."

"Pay attention, Shane. You are going to get lost," he said in his thick African accent.

He had *no* idea. She was already lost in her thoughts, her body, her everything. She didn't know how to log this feeling.

I'm a silly little girl, she thought, beating herself up for being so swept away.

But the feeling didn't fade. She searched the hallway for Coach after class, but he was nowhere in sight. By the time she went to lunch, she was distraught. She hadn't run into him again. And she *needed* to see him. She sat quietly, eating her food while Brandi and Marisa chatted away.

"Would you ever date a teacher?" she asked them, stopping their conversation in its tracks.

"No, and that's *so* gross," Brandi told her. "I knew you had a crush on Mr. Mutomba. I just knew it," she said through narrowed eyes.

"Shut up," Shane said, looking up from her link of boudain sausage. "Not him," she whispered.

"Well then, who?" Marisa asked, leaning in closer to her friend, intrigued by the question.

"Nobody. It was just a question. Forget about it."

Marisa and Brandi looked at each other, knowing that if they gave her a little time, she would tell them. They allowed the silence to hang in the air.

"I don't even know his name."

"So it is somebody, then," Marisa said. "Okay, junior year just got interesting. Your dad will kill you. You know that, right?"

"For real!" Brandi warned her. "Turn back now. Do not pass Go."

"Shut up, you two. I was in the hall, and I ran into what I thought was a student. I was all ready for him to put a ring on it *before* I knew he was a teacher. Life is so unfair."

"Two words: Councilman Foster. Just know this ... your daddy will not be happy if you get caught," Brandi laughed, shaking her head at the absurdity of what Shane was proposing.

"Bran's right, Shane. It cannot happen.

You have to get the dude out of your head. I heard old men have worms anyway. Ew."

"He's not old, dummy. He still looks like he's in high school. You're right about Daddy, though. I just have to forget about him. I'm never walking down that hallway again."

Shane passed down the front hallway at the end of the school day, avoiding her normal route to the gym. That way would have put her smack dab in front of the coach's classroom. She was still on a search to find the perfect outlet for herself for the school year. She wanted something new and fresh. Something she could conquer.

Earlier in the week, she found out that volleyball tryouts were coming up and decided to give it a shot. She was very athletic. Playing volleyball at the beach had always been fun for her. She decided it might be a good idea to try out for the team. If she was good enough, she could maybe play on the college level.

She joined the other girls, whom she recognized as players from last year. There were some new faces there, trying out for the JV squad, but the junior and senior varsity players were very familiar to her. When she spotted one of the girls from the journalism staff, she decided to sit with her. "Hey, Hannah," she said, sitting down on the bleachers.

"Hey, Shane! I didn't know you played volleyball." Hannah was a nice girl known around the newspaper staff for her athletic ability. She was white, with dark hair and eyes and an athletic body that gave other teams a run for their money.

"I love volleyball. I just never play at school. I just wanted something diff ... " her voice faded. Her mouth hung open.

"Are you okay?" Hannah asked her.

"Hey, ladies. Sorry I'm late. We had a quick meeting, but I'm here now."

Yes you are! Shane thought. It was him. He was the coach for the girls' volleyball team. There was nowhere to run now.

"I'm Coach Rob. This is my first year teaching and coaching, so you have to work with me on the learning curve."

"I'll help you with *whatever* you need," one of the girls said coyly.

Shane's head swung around to see who was flirting with him, but she caught herself. She knew she could not let anybody know how she was feeling about Coach Rob. The price was too great.

Once tryouts were done, Shane called her sister to come by the school and pick her up. While she was standing outside waiting for Robin, Coach Rob came out of his office to leave for the day.

"Good night, Shane," he said, passing her.

"Night, Coach," she said, trying to will him to turn around and talk to her.

"Shane," he said, walking back toward her.

Her heart was beating so fast. She was sure he could hear it. She swallowed hard. *Why does he have this effect on me?* "Yes?"

"You have a ride home, right? I'd hate to leave you out here alone. It's getting dark earlier and earlier these days."

"I'm fine," she said, cracking a smile. He was kind and considerate, not like the high school boys she knew.

"Well then, I'm going to wait with you. I need to get to know my players anyway."

"Players? I made the team?"

"Well, I can't tell you that just yet. You'll have to wait, but I will say that it's looking good. Very good." He winked at her, indicating she'd made the team. Yes!

They had a great conversation, talking like two old friends. She was surprised that he was so approachable. He was a grown-up, but their conversation felt natural. His voice touched her soul. Sitting on the steps so close to him was affecting her, and she wasn't ready for it to be over. When Robin's car pulled up in front of the gym, Shane was disappointed. "Well, that's my sister. Thanks for waiting with me."

"No problem. It was nice talking to you," he said, looking at her and making her knees go weak.

"Yeah, you too, Coach."

When she got in the car with Robin, she took a deep breath, allowing her head and body to finally relax.

"Who was the cutie?" Robin asked her.

"That's just the volleyball coach, Coach Rob."

"I was wondering why you were all of a sudden interested in volleyball," her sister said suspiciously. "You better be careful with that one, Shane. Don't get yourself into any trouble. I know that look in his eyes, and it's dangerous." Robin always gave her the best advice. The problem was that Shane usually didn't follow it.

"The look in his eyes? Did he look interested in me?" she asked excitedly.

"Shane," her sister warned, "you better not be thinking what I think you're thinking."

"I'm not thinking, Robin. That's the problem. He makes my mind go blank."

"Well, Daddy will make him go blank, so don't go there."

"Okay, okay ... you sound like Marisa and Brandi. I get it," she said, staring out the window, trying to push the thoughts of the new coach out of her head.

CHAPTER 7

Brandi

A normal Friday night for Brandi was anything but relaxing. It was usually filled with duties and responsibilities. That was part of the territory when you were the co-captain of a 5A cheerleading squad. This Friday night was the one night during football season that PCH didn't have a football game. Each school in the area had one Friday night off, and this was theirs.

Brandi decided to spend a little time with Dub at the studio and grab a bite to eat. Christina, one of the other cheerleaders on the squad, gave her a ride to the studio. She and Christina had been close ever since they roomed together at cheerleading camp Brandi's freshman year. Even though they didn't hang out much outside of cheerleading, they tried to make time for each other whenever their crazy schedules allowed.

"Hey, aren't you coming in?" she asked as Christina pulled up to the studio door without parking her car.

"Not tonight. But tell Dub I said hey. Y'all need some alone time. You need to figure out if you really want to be in a relationship with him," Christina told Brandi.

"You are always so wise."

"No, I just love my girl. You deserve to be happy, especially after everything ..." Christina had a hard time when Brandi was kidnapped. Shane and Marisa had each other, but she had felt really alone during those months. Being a year older than Brandi, Christina felt very protective of her. Dub seemed like a good dude. Christina just hoped he was sincere.

When Brandi entered the studio, she sat down in her spot next to Beaty at the boards. Dub's voice was coming through the speakers. "Hey, Bran," he said as she waved at him through the glass that separated the recording booth from the sound equipment.

Brandi played on her phone while listening to Dub as he put down another new hit. *He's so talented,* she thought. It was thirty minutes before she was even face-to-face with him. It would have been longer than that if Beaty hadn't received an urgent phone call and took off. When Dub came to meet her, he greeted her with a kiss. "Okay, so it seems my session just got canceled."

"Yeah, I can see that."

"What do you want to do tonight?"

"Nothing. Just chill," Brandi replied.

"Me too. Hey, I have an idea. Let's order

some pizza and watch a movie in the front office. There's a huge TV and couches. We don't even have to leave."

"That sounds great," she said.

After Dub ordered their pizzas, he found a movie that neither of them had seen. He dimmed the lights. They had their own private movie theater right there at the recording studio. Brandi nestled into the crevices of his body as he wrapped his arms around her. She hadn't been at peace with a guy in a long time. It was nice.

"Bran," he said, stroking her thick hair in his hands. "This is nice."

She looked up at him. "I was just thinking the same thing."

They were drawn to each other, as if a magnetic force pulled them together. There was no way she could move. Nor did she want to. Being in his arms felt safe. She welcomed his lips in an achingly sweet kiss. Her heart began to race. As soon as their lips touched, he adjusted his body.

Not even air could move between the two of them. His lips hungrily covered her face and neck. Then they heard the studio's door open abruptly.

"Devin! We need to talk!" Lil Flo yelled, interrupting their moment together.

"Whoa, Flo. Come on."

"Now, Devin."

"Hey, gimme a minute," Dub said, excusing himself.

Brandi was embarrassed to be busted in such a vulnerable position. *Yuck. I look like a studio groupie.* She sat, staring blankly at the TV, wondering what the big fuss was about. She could hear their raised voices through the wall. She knew that whatever was going on, it wasn't going well.

"It's not cool, Devin! You know what I'm going through! How could you?" Lil Flo seemed furious as she slammed the door to the studio, leaving negative energy in what had been a safe space.

"What was that about, *Devin*?" Brandi asked. She had grown upset listening to Lil Flo through the walls. She could have sworn that she heard her name.

"It's nothing, Brandi. Let me take you home."

"Oh, it's like that? She comes in here, throwing a fit, and you jump to take me home? Is there something that you want to tell me, Dub?"

He was quiet. He looked down at his feet as if they held the answers to his problems. "There's nothing to say."

"Christina will pick me up. I don't want your ride," she said as stormed out of the studio.

"It's dangerous out there, Brandi!" he yelled after her.

"Chris, I need a ride ... I don't know ... I have to get away from here, please ... I'm okay ... Just hurry." She was startled when she turned around to see Dub standing behind her. She wiped the tears from her eyes, trying to conceal her pain and fury.

"Bran, don't cry," he said, walking toward her. "It's complicated. Don't let what just happened taint what we have."

"Dub, we don't have anything if anybody can walk in here and make you jump through hoops. I wasn't looking for this, and I surely didn't ask for it."

"I'll make it up to you. I promise."

"You can't. It's already ruined," she said. "Christina is just down the road. She's gonna swoop me up. I can't even look at you right now."

"Please, Brandi—"

"Shut up. There's nothing you can say. Just. Shut. Up."

Dub stood there in silence.

Moments later, Brandi rushed to Christina's approaching car and got in. "Get me out of here, please."

CHAPTER 8

Ladies' Night

I need a night out," Shane said, adding the final touches to her makeup.

"Me too," Brandi admitted. "Where is Marisa? I thought she was going to meet us over here."

"She sent me a text earlier saying she would meet us out front at the Room."

"She doesn't seem like herself right now. I don't know what it is," Brandi said.

"To be honest with you, I think it's Trent. What else could it be?"

"Wouldn't she talk to us about it if it was just Trent?" Brandi asked.

"I don't know, B. You know Mari can be on hush mode sometimes. Let's get out of here. We won't be bumming rides pretty soon. I can't wait till you get your license."

When Brandi and Shane were dropped off at the Room, the first thing they did was look for Marisa. She told Shane she would meet them outside, but she was nowhere to be found. After sending her a text, she let them know she had already gone inside to party. When they walked in the door, they looked around for her, but she was still missing in action.

"Let's go to the restroom, maybe she'll meet us there," Brandi told Shane.

"Yeah, well, I'm starting to get worried. Something's fishy."

On the way to the restroom, they finally spotted Marisa on the dance floor. She was dancing with Brock, the quarterback for PCH. Marisa was draped all over him like they had been dating forever.

She was throwing herself at him, and he looked happy to play catcher.

"Shaaaane, Braaaan, my girls up in this piece," she said as they approached her. She was slurring her words terribly.

Both Shane and Brandi were horrified. They had never seen Marisa in this condition before. She gave them each a huge hug, and then she practically slid off her high heels, almost falling to the floor.

"Marisa, what's wrong with you?" Brandi asked between clenched teeth.

"Brock, you don't mind if we borrow Marisa for a second, do you?" Shane asked him.

"Nah, I'm just chillin'. But bring her back. We have some stuff to get into after this."

"Sure," Shane said, rolling her eyes at him. "Not in this lifetime, dude," she mumbled, helping Marisa to the restroom.

"Oh my God, it's Marisa," one girl exclaimed as they passed her. "The model."

Her friend knew exactly whom she was referring to. "Yeah. She's on the Wildcat's twirler squad. She's gonna get *so* busted. What's wrong with her?"

"We have to get her out of here," Brandi told Shane. "I think she might be drunk."

"And what tipped you off, Sherlock? I know she's drunk. Really drunk. I'm calling Robin right now. So much for our fun night out."

While Shane was dialing her sister's number, Brandi was struggling to keep Marisa on her feet. "I feel sick, Bran, so sick."

Marisa was in pretty bad shape. She started dry heaving like she was going to vomit, but nothing came up. She still looked beautiful even though she was a mess. Then next time she began to retch, Brandi got more than she bargained for. All over her new Bebe dress.

"Marisa!" Brandi screamed, trying to dodge the vomit that was coming directly her way, but she wasn't quick enough. They were both drenched in cheap alcohol and bile. "I'm going to kill you when you sober up."

Shane could not help but laugh. She couldn't believe her two BFFs were at the hottest teen club in Port City, covered in vomit. Marisa started to cry. Shane's laughter stopped immediately. "What's the matter, Mari?" Shane asked, going to her friend's side.

"He doesn't love me anymore." Her body slumped down onto the restroom floor. It was useless to try and pick her up. She was dead weight. They knew they had to get her out of there somehow, before the entire school learned she was a hot mess. Wrecked over a boy.

When a group of girls tried to get into the restroom, Shane slammed the door back on them. "This restroom is closed!

Come back later!" She turned her attention back to her friend. "Don't say that, Mari. I'm sure this is hard on Trent too."

Shane glared at Brandi with a look in her eyes that said *I told you*. This was the reason Shane did not give her heart to Ryan or Ashton the year before. No matter what promises they made to her, she knew it would end badly. She knew that they would move on with their lives and leave her behind in Port City.

Marisa, on the other hand, had leaped headfirst into her relationship with Trent. It seemed perfect at the time, but now here was the result. Marisa was drunk and practically unconscious on the bathroom floor at the Room.

"What are we going to do?"

"You get as much of that vomit off of the two of you as possible, and give that broad a peppermint," Shane growled. "Her breath is kicking. I'm going to get a little assistance. I'll get Robin to pull up to the back door."

Brandi worked feverishly to get them both cleaned up, but they still smelled like a dumpster full of rotting garbage. Just as she was done, Shane came busting through the door with their long-time friend, Matthew Kincade. If anybody was going to keep this on the hush, it was Matthew.

He had dated both Brandi and Marisa. As crazy as it sounded, Shane knew that he had loved them both. When she saw Mattie, she knew he was their guy. He swooped Marisa up in his arms. The girls followed him through an unused hall and out the back door. Matthew put Marisa in the backseat of Robin's car.

"Thanks, Mattie. I owe you one."

"Anytime, Shane. Hey, take care of her."

"You know I will."

Brandi gave her ex a crooked grin and shrugged her shoulders.

"Y'all stink," Robin told them, driving away from the Room. "I hope you have gas money too."

"Shut up, Robin. Drive—"

Before Shane could get more words out, Marisa was throwing up all over herself again and crying.

"I hate all of you," Robin said, staring blankly at the road. "You need to get this car cleaned and detailed. Or ... man, I hate y'all."

"Not true, sister. Not true at all," Shane said, planting a big kiss on her sister's cheek and laughing.

CHAPTER 9

Marisa

After the disaster of their ladies' night out, Marisa's goal was to focus on her modeling and schoolwork. Partying and carrying on had never been her thing. She had been fine before Trent had come into her life. She hadn't been looking for a relationship. It had just happened. Now, for some crazy reason, it left her feeling empty, alone, and depressed.

As she sat in class trying to focus, her mind drifted again to Trent and the girl who answered his dorm phone.

Focus, Marisa! Let him go.

She was finding it harder and harder to keep her grades up. Her parents had noticed her emaciated frame as her weight kept dropping. She tried to wear baggy clothing to hide her skinny bones. Her face looked gray. Her cheeks hollow. Her skin broke out. She did not look beautiful. She applied more and more makeup, trying to cover the flaws and sallow complexion.

Shane and Brandi were concerned about her. After all, they were the ones who really knew what was going on. After that dreadful Saturday night out, they started to question her.

When Marisa woke up at Shane's house on Sunday morning after ladies' night, her girls were sitting on the bed with breakfast and a hundred questions.

"Eat. Then we have to talk," Shane had told her.

"I can't eat. I feel sick," she had moaned.

But the girls would hear none of that.

They made her eat a piece of toast and drink some orange juice and coffee. It actually made her feel a little bit better. *Thank God for good friends.*

"What's up with you, Mari? You have to talk to us," Brandi said. The concern she felt for her friend hung in the room.

"I'm fine. I mean ... I will be fine."

"You are not fine, Marisa. I can't let you think you are fine. You didn't let me think I was fine when I was eating pills and smoking weed. So don't think you can get rid of me with 'I'm fine.'" Shane was the last person who Marisa could try to fool. Shane had already spiraled out of control during her freshman year. Luckily, her girls were there to pick her up when she hit rock bottom.

Marisa's eyes filled with tears. "Just give me some time. My head is killing me today. I promise. I'm going to get through this."

"Through what?" Brandi questioned.

Shane touched Brandi's arm, telling her friend to hold back.

"She'll talk to us when she's ready." She looked down at Marisa, who was reclining dramatically against some pillows. "We love you, Mari, and don't you forget it."

"I love you too. Now turn out the lights on your way to church. Please tell your mom I'm too sick to go. Please."

That had been a week ago. Now that it was time for another weekend. Marisa was no better off than she had been then. She still had not heard from Trent. She honestly believed that he would have called her back by now. No matter that when she called his cell phone, he sent her to voice mail. She had pleaded with him over text message to let her know he was okay, but she never got a response. *Coward! I hate him.*

Twirling was the only thing Marisa was excelling at. She had been voted feature twirler by the other girls on her squad, and she was actually enjoying all that came along with the title. She was given a solo performance at the home football games. Each time she went out to twirl, she put on a show.

This week she would be twirling her hoop baton that her sisters had made especially for her. It was decorated in royal blue, white, and silver. She practiced tricks that made the streamers and decorations dance as she sent the baton soaring through the air.

By the time Friday arrived, Marisa was finding pleasure in the thought of performing her solo on the field and revealing her new baton for all the PCH fans to see. For that moment, she was trying to put Trent out of her mind and enjoy high school.

"We should go out tonight after the game to celebrate our win, and we haven't officially welcomed the freshman twirlers either," she told the other twirlers as they warmed up.

They were a close squad, almost like family. Even Ashley, who had been her worst enemy for many years, was finally starting to come around. They managed to put a Band-Aid on their rocky relationship, even after Ashley threw herself at Trent the year before. It didn't sting so badly now, since he was all the way in Arkansas.

"We haven't even won the game yet," Bethany said.

"I know, but it does sound fun, right?"

"You know I'm always down for a reason to party, and it's my senior year. Count me in!" Taylor said.

She was the only senior on the twirling squad, which made her captain by default. She had always been a good twirler with strong basic skills. She was organized and dependable, but she wasn't the most talented. Her routines were sometimes boring, which made her the perfect captain. The glitz and glam was left to the feature twirler. That's where true skills were showcased.

"Hey, I'm in too," Ashley said, not about to let them leave her out. "And my mom is letting me use the car tonight, so it's on." Their impromptu night on the town was planned.

The girls met at Marisa's house after the game, each putting on their cutest and most comfortable parking lot pimping outfits. It was already eleven, so they were trying to get out of the house quickly. "Where is Ashley? She's always late," one of the freshman girls complained.

"Hey, I'll give her a call and make sure she's on her way," Taylor announced. They could always count on their captain to make sure everybody was where they were supposed to be, even on their chill nights.

Before Taylor could press Call, the doorbell rang and there was Ashley with party favors in hand. She held two clear bags with boxes of wine coolers. "Okay, now the party can begin."

"I don't drink," Bethany complained.

"Me neither, but I'm about to tonight," one of the other freshmen said, opening her first wine cooler.

"Wine coolers are weak," Ashley told them. "It'll just take the edge off, nothing major."

Marisa took her own wine cooler out of the bag. When Bethany saw her indulging, she decided that it might not be so bad to give it a try.

Once the girls were finished with their drinks, they snapped some pictures to add to their Friender pages and hit the road.

The night was filled with fun. By the time they arrived at the seawall, it was in full swing. They dropped the top of Ashley's mom's convertible and all eight girls piled in, parking Taylor's car at the entrance of the strip. They were looking good, feeling good, and ready to have some fun.

"Let's go find some cute boys! I want to flirt," Ashley said, trying to yell at them over the wind coming off the water.

As they rode down the seawall, finding cuties who could handle all eight of them was getting harder and harder. "Dang, girl, swing that car over!" one guy yelled as he hung out of his friend's ride.

"Boy, we rollin' deep. Y'all can't handle all this." The girls laughed at them for even trying to holler.

"Hey, I thought he was cute," Bethany said, wanting to go back.

"Were they on the field tonight?" Ashley asked her.

"I don't think so."

"Well, then we ain't interested. I'm going to where the football team hangs, and that's the only place I'm stopping."

When they got to the football team's usual turf, it was packed with females.

They were all starstruck by the unde-
feated Port City High football team. It was
easy to be smitten. There were muscles
bulging out of shirts all over that section
of the pier. Some guys just went shirtless
altogether. Clothes were always optional
at the seawall.

"Marisa Maldonado," she heard a voice
say. "You're not with your normal crew
tonight, huh?" It was Matthew Kincade.

"Hey, Mattie. Nah, we are taking the
freshman twirlers out tonight."

"Oh yeah, hey, hook me up with your
girl Bethany." Matthew was always trying
to get with somebody. It was just him.
Marisa had almost fallen for his lines
in ninth grade. Luckily, she dodged that
bullet.

"Bye, Mattie," she said, walking away.
"And thanks for the save the other night!"
she yelled back.

"Anytime, but don't make a habit of it!"
He shook his finger at his friend.

Her little buzz was starting to slip away. She looked at the other twirlers who were having a great time. She was so happy that she had planned an outing for them.

"Mari!" Bethany yelled. "You think we can meet the team at Waffle House? They just invited us."

Marisa was so tired after the game and their outing, but she didn't want to be a party pooper, so she agreed. Bethany was so excited. How could Marisa refuse? They went to the entrance of the seawall and divided up between cars. "Shot gun!" Bethany yelled, jumping into the car with Ashley.

"I'm rolling with Taylor. It's the Waffle House by the mall," Marisa yelled to them. They pumped up the new Young Dub CD and just zoned out. The two freshman girls who rode with Taylor and Marisa put their windows down and sat on the doors to catch the last bit of air before leaving the dock.

"Y'all heifers are crazy. I'm gonna get a ticket. Sit down!" Taylor yelled, looking through her rearview mirror. She could have sworn she saw police lights. The car swerved as she tried to get the girls in her car under control.

"Taylor!" Marisa screamed. Taylor had almost hit two girls in a crosswalk.

"Oh my God, I didn't see them at all. Thanks, Marisa."

Marisa looked back to make sure that they were okay. "No prob—" she started to say. But before the words could leave her lips, there was a loud crunch. Their car had clipped Ashley's car, startling them.

"Oh my—Taylor, turn the wheel, turn the wheel!" Marisa reached over and grabbed the wheel of Taylor's car, trying to steer her away from Ashley's ride. This maneuver sent Taylor's car toward a tree in the median. It was impossible to miss. Without wearing a seatbelt, Marisa's body flew from her seat. She slammed into the windshield.

Ashley's car spun out of control. When it finally came to a halt on the other side of the street, bystanders ran to help. Everyone was thankful it hadn't been worse. More people were coming down from the seawall to help. Out of nowhere, a truck came barreling down the road. The truck's driver never saw Taylor's car in the median, or the students running toward the truck, warning it to stop. The truck hit Ashley's car head on.

CHAPTER 10

Brandi

The football game had worn Brandi out. The only thing she wanted to do was go home, get a bath, and spend some quality time with Raven. After they finished watching *Sparkle* for the twentieth time, Raven was ready to plop down on her sister's bed for a little more time with her.

"RaRa, I need a little time to myself tonight. I had fun with you, though."

"I love it when you spend time at home, Bran. We should do movie night every night," she said, giving her sister a huge hug.

"Well, I don't know about every night. I have a lot of things that I'm responsible for. You'll see how it is when you get to high school. Now go get some sleep. I'll see you in the morning."

Raven was quite possibly Brandi's favorite person in the whole world. She loved her best friends, but her little sister was the love of her life. Brandi had begged her mom and dad to have a baby for years before they finally announced her mom was pregnant. She was six years old at the time, but she remembered it like it was yesterday. She was so happy that she would have a sibling.

The day Brandi found out she was going to have a sister, the Haywoods thought she would jump out of her skin. From the moment Raven was born, she took care of that little girl the best she could. She was a partner in everything, the good and the bad.

When Brandi had been kidnapped by

her childhood friend's brother, it was Raven who never stopped looking for her. It was Raven who came up with the plan to save her. She had only been eight years old at the time, but she was the bravest, smartest, and funniest kid that Brandi had ever seen.

Their father's drug addiction had brought them closer. Brandi was super protective of Raven. She didn't want her making the same mistakes that Brandi had made growing up.

Brandi had been watching over Raven her entire life, making sure all her needs were met. It was a big job for any sibling, but she had been willing to do whatever was necessary to ensure that her little sister was fed, clean, and happy. Because of this, Raven was a mellow fifth grader. Their family was lucky. Their father had beat his drug addiction. The hard part was behind them.

Brandi relaxed on her bed, thinking of those tough years and feeling blessed.

She knew her family had turned a corner, and she was thankful. The weight of the world was no longer on her shoulders. She decided to check her Friender page before trying to get some sleep. It was already one o'clock in the morning, and it had been a long day.

Online, she looked at the graphic photos of the mangled cars by the seawall. *Oh my God. Is that Port City?* She examined the pictures closely. She couldn't even tell what kind of cars were in the pictures. One caption even stated that the accident was so bad a girl had died. Nobody knew the victim's name in all of the mayhem.

She grabbed her phone to send Shane and Marisa a text. She was sure they were both in bed already. Neither of them had plans to go out. Shane's whole family was out of town, so she had opted for a quiet night at home. She knew Marisa had planned to go home after the game since her horrible weekend last week.

"I'm just glad my friends are home and safe," she said aloud. Neither of them responded, but she took that as a good sign. *They must be asleep already.* She tried to investigate, but none of her close friends were online.

She decided to call Christina. She was always awake for some odd reason. When Christina answered the phone, there was so much noise that Brandi couldn't hear what she was saying. But she could tell that Christina was crying.

Brandi started to panic. *Oh my God. Christina must have been hurt.* She wanted to get to the accident site. But the online news said there was no way in and no way out. She needed Christina to calm down and talk to her.

"Chris, you have to tell me what's going on!" she yelled. "Snap out of it."

"They've been badly hurt, Bran. You have to get to the hospital." Christina was frantic and yelling.

"Who's hurt, Chris?" She could hear sirens in the background. She couldn't make out what was being said. Christina was talking to someone. Brandi pressed her ear to the phone as hard as she could, trying to hear anything that would help her understand what was happening.

"Hold on, Mari. We don't want to move you. The EMTs are going to get you out. You have to hold on."

Brandi dropped the phone. The face of her cell phone shattered and the screen turned blue. She tried to hit it against her hand to get it to come back on, but it was in reset mode. *Crap. No, oh my God.* Hopefully it would power back up later, but that wouldn't help her now. She tried to get down the stairs to her parents' room. She slid down most of the way, losing her balance in the dark.

"Mama!" she yelled. "Mama!"

She woke the whole house up. Her

mom, her dad, and a frightened Raven, who came running to her aid.

"Mama, there's been an accident. There's been an accident. I have to go!" Brandi screamed. She was sobbing and collapsed in her mother's arms.

"Who, baby? What's wrong? Talk to me." She looked at her husband for help. They didn't know what was happening. "You have to tell me what's going on." She was becoming frustrated. The nurse in her wanted to get to the problem, but her daughter wasn't helping her figure it out.

Finally, through her tears, Brandi was able to speak. "It's Mari. I have to go. I have to get to her." She released her mother and ran back up the stairs. "I'm going to put some clothes on. I have to call Shane. Oh my God. Help us. Mom, please drive me to the hospital."

CHAPTER 11

Shane

Friday night had never felt so good before. Shane had spent the entire evening doing absolutely nothing. She was supposed to be at the football game taking yearbook pictures and cheering their team, but she just couldn't, not tonight. She started feeling ill during the day and made a quick excuse for her absence. Mrs. Monroe was very understanding and released her from her obligations. "I hope you feel better, Shane. Have a good weekend."

"You too, Mrs. Monroe." Her whole family had planned a trip out of town.

Normally that meant she would either have to stay with Marisa or Brandi, but they were both at the game. She assured her parents that she would be fine staying by herself. They finally relented and allowed her to stay home.

"No funny business, Shane. Stay away from Riley, and don't have any boys in my house." Riley had been Shane's smoking buddy and partner in crime when she was acting out. Her family had forgiven Riley after Shane's out-of-control spiral freshman year, but they still didn't think their relationship was a healthy one.

"Dad, I'm about to take some NyQuil and go to bed. I need to catch up on *Dallas* anyway."

"Watch the History Channel or something productive," her dad replied.

"You know that's not going to happen, right? Now go. I need to get some rest."

She had fallen asleep trying to get caught up on her favorite show. When she woke up, it was already eight o'clock in the morning. All she wanted to do was get some orange juice, a piece of toast, and go back to bed. She took out her phone to see if her family had called. She hadn't heard from them at all, which wasn't normal. "Shoot, my phone is dead. No wonder," she said aloud.

After she plugged in her phone, she took out her laptop and opened her Friender page. "What's happening in the real world?" She knew all of her friends were still asleep. She had slept for twelve hours and was about to sleep some more after getting caught up on the Friday night gossip and talking to her family.

As soon as she opened her page, she started to see pictures from an accident that happened after the game. "Oh my goodness, a PCH student was killed last night. That's crazy!"

As soon as her phone charged enough to receive messages, it started chiming.

There was beep after beep coming in, indicating that there had been a lot of activity while it was dead. "Who's texting me like that?"

She couldn't take her eyes off the pictures on the Internet to check her phone. "This is some crazy stuff." Then her eyes fell on the caption. She couldn't believe what she was reading. "RIP Marisa Maldonado—You will be missed." She was in a daze. She felt herself reacting. She ran to the phone. Mari must have called her. This was a sick joke. There was no way ...

There was no call from Mari. It was Brandi who was blowing up her phone. "Plz call me S. we hafta talk."

"No, no, no!" she screamed. "Stupid phone. Stupid. Stupid. Why didn't I charge it?" She called Brandi's phone. "Bran!" she yelled frantically.

Brandi's voice was hoarse when she answered her. "Where have you been, Shane? I've been trying to reach you."

"Bran, somebody has put some really foul stuff on Friender about Mari. I read on the Internet that she's dead. That's just crazy, right?" There was silence on the other end as Brandi tried to compose herself. "Bran, talk to me, and you talk to me now."

"She's not dead, Shane. She made it, but ..." Brandi had been crying all night. She was trying to hold it together, but talking to Shane for the first time just brought all those feelings back to the surface.

"But? There's no but. She's not dead. Oh my God, what a relief." Shane fell down in the chair at her desk, relieved. She had been pacing frantically around her bedroom.

"But she's in critical condition. They don't know if she's going to make it. We've already lost Bethany."

"What? Wait ... lost Bethany? What does that mean?"

"Shane, they pronounced her dead when she got to the hospital. It's been a long night. Are you coming to the hospital? I need you to be here."

"I don't have a ride. My whole family is gone. Gavin even went with them. He and Aiden went with Robin in her car." Shane started to cry. Her whole body went limp. She was alone. She tried to pull herself together. "Look, I'll be there. If I have to call a taxi, I'll be there. Just tell Marisa I'm coming, please."

"She won't be able to—"

"Just tell her I'm coming!" Shane shouted. She tried to calm herself down. "Please, Brandi. Just tell her."

She called everybody she knew but couldn't find a ride. She didn't want to get a taxi. Taxi drivers made her nervous, and she was nervous enough. She even knocked on the door of the old lady who lived across the street. She wasn't home.

After one more crying spell, Shane

pulled herself together and started going through her phone again. She called her mom and dad, but they didn't answer either. "I need help!" she screamed. Then she saw the paper on the floor from volleyball practice. "Coach Rob."

She picked up her cell phone and dialed.

"Hello?" a masculine voice said.

"Coach? Hey, it's Shane. Shane Foster."

"Shane, what's the matter?"

"There's been an accident. My parents are out of town. I need help." She started to cry again, even though she tried to will herself not to.

"You were in an accident? Are you okay?"

"No, not me. Marisa. I just need a ride to the hospital. Can you help me?"

"Yes. I'm on my way. Text me your address."

She sent him her address and put on a pair of sweats and a T-shirt. She pulled her hair into a ponytail and brushed her teeth. She sat on her porch, waiting for Coach Rob to get there.

What's taking him so long? she thought. She went to the end of the sidewalk to see if his car was approaching. She didn't even know what he drove. There wasn't a car in sight. She went back to the porch and sat on the swing. "Come on, Coach." Tears welled in her eyes. She didn't notice when Coach Rob's car finally approached the house.

"Shane! Come on, let's get you there," he said as he walked to help her into his Camaro. It wasn't exactly the car Shane had expected. It was so hot. She pictured them cruising the seawall together, enjoying a beautiful, sunny day in Texas with the breeze blowing through the windows. *Stop it. Marisa may be dying, and you're focused on Coach Rob.*

"Are you okay?"

"I will be better when I get to Marisa."

CHAPTER 12

Broken

As soon as Coach Rob's car pulled up to the door of the hospital, Shane jumped out of the car and thanked him. She couldn't waste any more time getting to her best friends. She knew Marisa was still in dangerous territory. According to Brandi, she had sustained a serious head injury, and everyone was on close watch, hoping for the best.

"Shane! Are you going to be okay?" he yelled from the car, but the emergency room doors closed quickly behind her. She never looked back.

The hospital was big and confusing. She had entered through the emergency room door—the last place to get help quickly. The staff barely had time to blink, much less look up the name of a patient.

When she finally made it to the reception area, she was ready to scream. "Miss, can you help me? I need to find someone. Marisa Maldonado. She was in an accident last night." It was only nine in the morning, and it seemed as if she had lived a whole day since her eyes opened that morning. So much had changed overnight.

The receptionist looked in the computer to find Marisa's name. "She's in the intensive care unit on the second floor. Use those elevators in the lobby," she said, pointing her in the right direction.

Everything was moving too slow for her, even elevators. "Come on, come on."

"Shane? Shane!" Brandi said, running to her friend and hugging her tightly as Shane entered the ICU's waiting room.

"How is she?"

"Last I heard, she was doing better, but her head hit the windshield hard, so they have to monitor her closely. She's heavily sedated. She doesn't even know when I'm in the room." Brandi started to cry again. Her eyes were puffy and red from the lack of sleep and the constant tears.

"Can I go in and see her?" Shane asked.

"Mi hija," Mrs. Maldonado said, coming around the corner. "We tried to reach you all night."

"I'm sorry, Mrs. M. I should have been here. I was sick and took some NyQuil. I didn't know," Shane cried, hugging Mrs. Maldonado. The rest of the family was not far behind her. Marisa's little sisters and brother looked as bad as Brandi. They were all very solemn. "Is there any news yet? Is she going to be okay?"

"She doesn't look good, Shane. We feel so bad for Bethany's family. She was such a sweet girl. I can't believe she's gone. Marisa doesn't know yet, so when you go in there, please don't mention anything."

"Can she hear me?"

"We think so."

Shane waited for the time when visitors were allowed in the ICU. Everyone decided to let her go in to see Marisa first. A patient was only allowed two visitors at a time, so Brandi went in with Shane. When they got to the door of her room, Shane wasn't prepared for the amount of bandages on Marisa's face. She held tightly to Brandi. There was no way to prepare her brain for what she was about to see.

"Hey, Mari, it's us," Shane said. Tears poured from her eyes uncontrollably. "I'm so sorry I'm late." Shane rubbed Marisa's hand so that she could know they were there. "Brandi's here too."

"Hey, Mari," Brandi said, moving to the other side of the bed. "You're probably tired of me coming in here." She laughed nervously.

They only stayed for a few minutes. They wanted to leave enough time for her family to come in and visit too. They went down to the cafeteria to get some juice and split a bagel.

Hours went by. One of the ICU nurses came to the waiting room to give the family an update. The hospital had decided to start reducing Marisa's pain medication so that she could start waking up. They wanted to keep her still as much as possible to prevent any more injuries to her head, but they also wanted to get her functioning as quickly as possible. The doctors decided to gradually take her off the meds so that her system wouldn't be shocked.

When nightfall came and there was no change in her condition, Brandi and Shane decided to go home and get cleaned up. Thankfully, the Fosters had returned from their trip to Austin and came to get them. Both the Haywoods and the Fosters were distraught. Marisa was like a daughter to them too.

Mrs. Foster hugged her daughter tightly. Shane broke down in her mother's arms. "Does Lupe need anything?" Mrs. Foster had asked, wiping the tears from her daughter's face.

"No, I don't think so."

"Brandi, how's your mom holding up?"

"She's on duty now. You know she can't help but be at the hospital as much as possible. She doesn't work in the ICU, but they've been allowing her to keep a close eye on Marisa."

Mrs. Foster forced them to eat some homemade chicken noodle soup before driving them back to the hospital. It was late, but they wanted to see Marisa one more time before bed. Robin would pick them up.

When they went up to the ICU, there were no Maldonados anywhere. "Where do you think they are?" Brandi asked.

One of the family members of another ICU patient responded. "They took that young girl to a regular room. The doctors said that she was doing a lot better."

"That's great news. Let's go find our girl." They ran to the help desk to get her room number.

When they got to Marisa's new room, they were more than happy to realize her eyes were open. The doctor's plan to wake her up had worked. Her face and arms were heavily bandaged, but there were a lot fewer machines. And she was trying to speak. Her eyes softened when her friends walked in the room. Though in an instant, she changed. Her body language showed her pulling away from them. It was an odd reaction to seeing her best friends.

Everyone excused themselves to let the girls talk for a bit.

"Hey," Marisa said hoarsely, studying the hospital gown she wore.

"It is so good to see your face," Brandi said.

"Some face," Marisa answered slowly.

"Girl, please, those scars will heal. You are beautiful inside and out."

Marisa shook her head. Tears seemed to jump from her eyes. "My fault," she tried to will her voice to speak.

"It is not your fault, baby girl. There was no way to know this was going to happen."

She began to cry. "Please go." She turned away from them, burying her face in the pillows. "Please, I can't do this."

CHAPTER 13

Brandi

*W*hat was that? I've been here all night, and she doesn't even want to see me?" Brandi couldn't believe what she was hearing.

"Brandi, she's going through something," Shane said. "It started well before this accident. I told you something was up with Mari. Now you see, right? That wasn't like Marisa at all."

"Why does she think that this is her fault? It's not like she was driving."

"I don't know. Sometimes a person can be in so much pain they don't think rationally. Trust me, I know." Shane remembered back to her own struggles. She was not willing to tell her friends when she was in trouble. She knew how difficult it was to look vulnerable.

"You're preaching to the choir. It's not like I haven't known my share of struggle. If only I had listened to my friends when I was dating that creep on Friender, I would have never put myself in a position to be kidnapped. I mean ... I get it. I just wanted to be there for Mari like she's been there for me. And let's not even talk about Bryce."

"Ugh. Me too, Brandi, but we can't save each other from making mistakes. What we have to do is be there when she's trying to make sense of all this. She's gonna need us."

Robin was there to pick them up when they left the hospital. Mrs. Foster was watching Aiden, Robin's son, so they decided to take a ride and clear their heads. They headed to the seawall. They knew their other friends would be hanging out there.

When the got there, they saw flowers covering the area of the accident. There was a photograph of Bethany. And lots of burning candles. Groups of students stood around, chatting and crying.

"I've decided not to get my driver's license just yet. I don't feel like driving anymore," Brandi announced, staring at the students as they mourned.

"This is very sad," Robin said as her car pulled up. "I don't think I can stay here."

"Let's just go by the studio. I can't cry anymore, Shane," Brandi told them.

The studio wasn't far from the seawall, so they went to see Dub and Beaty. Hopefully, Beaty had some jokes and would break the mood. When they got to the studio, the door was unlocked. Beaty's car wasn't in the parking lot. Only Flo and Dub's vehicles were there.

"Are you sure it's okay if we stop by without calling?" Robin asked her.

"I come here all the time," Brandi told her. "It's like my second home. I never call first. Plus, Dub knows we are going through it right now. He's like a brother to Marisa."

Flo and Dub never heard them walking into the studio. They probably both thought the door was locked. And Brandi was totally unprepared for what she saw. They were in the recording booth together, but there was no music going on. Brandi was frozen where she stood.

Lil Flo and Dub were passionately making out, like it wasn't the first time. Dub had been adamant that there was nothing going on between him and Flo. But Brandi knew something was suspicious about Flo's hatred toward her, and now she knew why.

"Bran. Brandi, let's go," Shane tried to nudge her friend.

Brandi waved her off. No way was she going down without a fight. Brandi pressed a button on the boards, and her voice came alive in the recording booth. "Dub! Really? That's why that skank was trippin'. I knew it!" she screamed.

"Who dat no name broad talkin' about? Check yo girl, Devin, before I have to!"

"*You* check me! Space and opportunity, Flo!" The situation was quickly getting out of control.

Brandi stormed out of the studio with Shane and Robin close behind. Flo started to go after her, but Dub made her stay put. He ran out to catch up to Brandi. "Brandi, wait! Come on, Brandi! Please," he pleaded. He tried to stop her, but she just shook her head. A tear rolled from her eye. She had almost given in to Dub. She had almost believed she was special. That she would be enough for him.

"Let her go, Devin!" Flo yelled as she barged out of the studio door. "She don't know you like I do anyway. It was time for her to step!"

"I told you to stay inside, Flo!" He grabbed Brandi's arm. "I'm so sorry, Brandi." She didn't look at him, but she didn't move either. "It's not like we were in a relationship. We were just kicking it, right?"

She looked at him. She barely recognized the person in front of her. Her eyes were cold. "Right. Good-bye, Dub." She kissed him on the cheek and got into the car. It was over. Before it had even started, really.

"Are you okay?" Shane asked her, but Brandi didn't respond. "B, say something."

"I'm fine, Shane. Okay? I wasn't supposed to be dating anyway. This is my fault. I let him get too close. I almost fell for the stupid limos, backstage passes, chillin' at the studio ..." her voice trailed off. She turned to look back at Dub as the car pulled away. He never moved. "Marisa is my only concern right now. That's what really matters."

"You're right, and we need to go see Bethany's family in the morning. Marisa would want us to do that."

They rode in silence for the rest of the ride home. It had been a long weekend. And it wasn't over yet.

CHAPTER 14

Shane

On Sunday, Shane and Brandi went back to the hospital to check on Marisa. When they arrived at her room, her mother was on her way out. Mrs. Maldonado's eyes were red and puffy. It looked as though she'd been crying for days.

"Mrs. M? Is Marisa okay?" Shane asked, concerned.

"She's not really talking anymore. We can't seem to get through to her. She looked in the mirror for the first time today. When my baby saw her face, she lost it. She hasn't spoken since."

"Is it a good time for us to go in?" Brandi asked.

"You can try, but don't expect too much."

They slowly opened the door to her hospital room. It was dark and cold. The only signs of life were the bouquets of flowers from her agent, the photographers she had worked with, and her friends. Brandi sat to Marisa's left. Shane to her right. Marisa turned toward Brandi, burying her face into her pillow. Brandi reached out and touched her hand, but Marisa quickly pulled away from her. Her quick reaction caught Brandi off guard, and she pulled away too.

"How are you?" Shane asked her, trying to talk to her.

After what seemed like forever, Marisa cleared her throat to speak. "Bethany," was all she could get out. The tears started to pour from her eyes. "It hurts to talk," she said hoarsely. The stitches on her face held it in the same position, making it difficult to communicate.

"Don't talk, Marisa. We'll just be here."

"No," she said quickly. "I'm hideous." The tears kept coming, like an emotional faucet had been turned on.

"You are not hideous. You will heal in no time," Shane tried to tell her.

Marisa searched the ceiling for answers. After a moment, she told them she wanted to be alone, and they obliged. They decided it was time to pay their respects to Bethany's parents. They both knew it would be hard, but it's what Marisa would have wanted them to do.

Brandi and Shane were surprised when they walked through the door. There were many other PCH students packed into Bethany's home already. They went through the process of speaking, hugging, and consoling. Bethany's mother came out of the kitchen with a tray of sandwiches. She was trying to stay busy and take her mind off her daughter's death.

When she saw Shane and Brandi, she started to cry. "She truly looked up to the two of you. Marisa was her idol. She wanted friends just like you." Mrs. Thomas lost it. Her husband rushed to her side to try and console her. "Please excuse me," she said, retreating up the stairs.

By the time they left the Thomas's house, they were exhausted. It was time to start getting ready for school the next day. Neither of them wanted to go. They both knew they would miss Marisa too much.

Just as they had anticipated, the whole school was talking about the accident. There was a moment of silence for Bethany, and a prayer was said for Marisa. All the other twirlers had escaped with minor scrapes and bruises, but they were still absent.

By the end of the day, Shane felt like she had been on a roller coaster. She didn't know how to feel or what to say when people asked about Marisa.

After volleyball practice, she sat on the bleachers and could not compose herself. She was alone, so she let her emotions flow freely. She was tired of being strong. She had been so vulnerable on the inside all day, and now it was over. She cried for Bethany and Marisa. In that moment, it was as if she could feel her friend's pain. She never heard the gym door open, but she did feel the hand on her shoulder.

"I'm sorry. I was just leaving." She began to gather her belongings. She was embarrassed. How long had this person been there? She wanted to separate herself from the situation as quickly as possible.

"Hey, it's okay." She was sure that it had been the janitor coming in to clean the gym, but instead it was Coach Rob.

She melted under his grasp. "Coach." She was relieved it was him. She felt comfortable enough to let go. After all, he was the one who had brought her to the hospital to check on her friend. They hadn't spoken since. "Thanks ... for everything," she said, studying her feet. The tears had caused her eyes to glaze over. She couldn't even look at him.

When she stood up to leave, Coach Rob touched her chin gently and wiped the tears from her face. His kindness made her start to cry again. "I swear I don't cry this much in real life."

He put his finger to her lips. "It's okay. I would cry too." He was so sincere. He pulled her close to him, just like her dad did when she was little, but there was nothing fatherly about his embrace. Her whole body awakened to his touch.

She finally looked into his eyes. She had to know if it was just her, or if he felt the same thing she did. The electricity of their touch could not be denied. She stood on her toes, grabbed the back of his head, and began to kiss him. At first it was gentle, but it quickly turned passionate. All of the feelings she had suppressed came to the surface. She pressed her body into his as though he was the therapy for her pain.

"Shane," he said, pulling away from her. "I can't."

She was so embarrassed. "Oh my God. What have I done?" She tried to run away from him. She tried to gather the few things she had brought to the gym, but she dropped them. Coach Rob bent down to help her pick them up. It was reminiscent of the first time they met. He grabbed her arm.

"Shane. Stop."

She felt her body give in to his touch. She tried to avoid his gaze. She couldn't believe that she had kissed a teacher. *Who does that?* she thought.

"Shane, I know I shouldn't say this, but you shouldn't feel bad." He paused as if he was choosing his words carefully. "I wanted to kiss you too."

CHAPTER 15

Marisa

Weeks passed but Marisa had still not gone back to school. She couldn't confront the fact that Bethany was dead. She didn't want anybody to look at the scars on her face. In her mind, she had gone from the It Girl in Port City to being a monster. She hated mirrors and refused to look at them. When she was released from the hospital, she took down all the mirrors in her room and in her bathroom. She was ruined.

Her agent tried feverishly to contact her, but Marisa could not see the point.

Why do I need to talk to her? So she can tell me my modeling career is over?

When Trent found out about the accident, he got in his car and drove for ten hours to get to Marisa, but she refused to see him. *You're too late, Trent, way too late,* she thought as she listened to her mother telling him that she didn't want visitors. He had pleaded with her. He didn't care how she looked, he needed to see her. He wanted to see for himself that she was okay.

No amount of pleading would have brought Marisa out of her bedroom. She didn't even want her own family to look at her face. The only person allowed in her room was her mother. She angered her father each day by locking her door and not letting anyone in.

"It's not normal for a girl to shut the world out, mi hija," he said one day, beating on her bedroom door.

"Go away, Papa. I just can't come out."

"Give her time, George," her mother had said. "It's only been a few weeks."

He relented and let Marisa heal, but he didn't want to. He wanted to rescue his baby girl from the pain, but she wasn't ready.

Marisa sat in her room and completed her assignments from school. Shane and Brandi came by each day to bring her schoolwork. "Is she in the mood for company yet?" Brandi asked Mrs. Maldonado.

"Not today, Brandi. She just needs some time."

"You can't hide in there forever, Mari! You have to come out at some point!" Shane yelled, knowing that Marisa could hear her. But it wasn't enough to get a response.

The girls were persistent, but they knew Marisa could be stubborn when she wanted to be. She wasn't giving in. She peeked through the blinds and watched as her two best friends retreated. Defeated once again.

"I love you both," she said, kissing her hand and pressing it against her window. She slid down to the floor and began to cry. She had cried so many tears in the past month. She didn't even know if she had the capacity to shed even more, but there they were.

When she picked herself up off the floor, she looked in the small, broken mirror she used to examine her scars. She massaged the scar tissue and rubbed vitamin E all over it. She didn't know if she was imagining things or not, but the scars seemed to have faded considerably. *I'm just getting used to them,* she thought sourly.

There was a knock on the door. She quickly looked out the window to see who was there, but she didn't recognize the car. She jumped into bed and pulled the covers over her head, trying to drown out the voices seeping through the walls.

She couldn't make out what was being said. There were whispers, and it annoyed her. She wanted the world to go away. She wanted to disappear. One month after the accident and she still felt the same way.

The guilt of the crash weighed heavily on her. She was sure she could live with the scars, but Bethany's death had changed everything. She had nightmares about that night. Sometimes she was lucky and her mind would change the outcome.

There was a knock on her door. "Mi hija, it's Mama," her mother said gently and entered her room. Marisa never pulled down her covers. "There's someone here to see you, mi hija."

Marisa ignored her mother. She wasn't coming out for anybody, not Shane, not Brandi, not Trent. "Mari, Bethany's mother came to see you. You have to talk to her. She's hurting more than you are. Now clean yourself up because I'm sending her in soon."

Marisa pulled herself out of bed and showered. It had been days since she had bathed, and she didn't want to offend Mrs. Thomas. She pulled on her Pink brand sweats that her mom had bought from Victoria's Secret in an attempt to cheer her up. When she was done, she opened the door to her bedroom without saying a word. She sat on her bed, waiting.

Mrs. Thomas entered. She looked at the pictures in Marisa's room without speaking to her. She took one of the photos from Marisa's dresser. It was the one of Marisa and Bethany at twirling camp.

"She looks so happy."

"She was," Marisa said, smiling for one second. She felt guilty. She knew Bethany would never smile again.

"Yeah, you're right. She was a happy girl. Are you happy, Marisa?" she asked as she sat down on the bed next to her. Marisa didn't answer the question. Instead, she played with a thread that was unraveling from her comforter. "You don't have to answer me. I know you're not happy. Your mother and I talk frequently now. She feels like she lost you the day of the accident. Like I lost Bethany." She paused, allowing her words to sink in. "But you're not dead, Marisa. Bethany is. I know my daughter better than anyone. She would never have wanted this life for you. Never."

Marisa sat with her knees bent. Her elbows rested on them. After Mrs. Thomas's speech, her head fell to her arms. The all too familiar tears began to fall again. She shook her head. She couldn't find words.

"It's time, Marisa. You have to let go of the guilt. You have to let Bethany go. She will always be with us. She has to live through us, but she can't live if we don't. Now come here." She pulled Marisa into her arms like she had done when Bethany was sad. Marisa continued to cry, but with each tear, she felt a little bit stronger. She knew Mrs. Thomas was right.

Mrs. Thomas took her by the chin and examined her face. "It looks like you'll be modeling in no time, beautiful girl. Now it's time to come out of this room. It's time to go back to school. Let the pain drive you forward, not hold you back." She took Marisa by the hand. "Come on. Let's show your family you are okay. They've been worried sick about you."

Marisa allowed Mrs. Thomas to walk her into the living room. She couldn't believe she had given in to her, but here she was. She couldn't lie. It felt good to be out of her room.

"Mi hija," her father gasped. He hugged her so hard she thought she would break. She smiled in his arms.

"I'm going to go now, Lupe." Mrs. Thomas turned back to Marisa. "Come see me some time."

Marisa hugged her tightly. "For sure," she said, and she meant it.

CHAPTER 16

Thanksgiving Breakup

Marisa had been back at school for only a week when it was time for Thanksgiving break. She had not expected the support she'd received from her classmates. When she got out of the car, Mrs. Monroe was there to greet her. "Good morning, Marisa."

"Good morning, Mrs. Monroe," she said, prepared to walk right past her.

"Marisa, can you join me in my class-room for a second before you go to the cafeteria?" She followed Mrs. Monroe silently. She really didn't know what to expect from her first day back. Mrs. Monroe's presence had caught her off guard. When she entered the classroom, Shane and Brandi were already there with her favorite breakfast from Starbucks and a grande chai tea latte.

"Welcome back," they both said, giving her tight hugs.

"We couldn't let you walk into school alone," Brandi told her as Shane stepped into the hallway, ushering in the twirling squad who had missed their feature twirler tremendously. Marisa was overwhelmed with emotion.

"I thought that you were all going to be mad at me," she said, holding on to the warm cup and smelling the pepper and cinnamon, as if the aroma was giving her strength.

"Are you serious?" Ashley asked her. "We all felt so bad about everything that you went through. I'm so sorry, Mari." Ashley began to cry. Ashley had beaten herself up for weeks, since she was the one who had introduced alcohol into their girls' night. She thought that one wine cooler each couldn't have caused the tragedy, but it made all of them question themselves and feel even guiltier.

"Don't cry, Ash. No more tears. None of us are to blame. I realize that now. It was just an accident. I'm still coming to grips with the fact that it left me looking like a freak."

"Marisa, you do not look like a freak," Mrs. Monroe stepped in. "You have a few scars from this accident, but trust me, those will fade. You are a beautiful girl."

Marisa began to cry. "Oh my God ... no more tears ... no more tears." She tried to blink away her pain, but tears fell down her cheeks anyway.

Taylor was by her side in seconds. "I take the blame for the whole thing. I know that you are trying to be kind, but you don't have to. I know I'm responsible for Bethany's death and for your ..." Taylor was a mess. Marisa was just realizing that they were all a mess. She had been so selfish. She had hidden out in her room while her friends were suffering as much as she was. She knew she should have been there with them.

They gathered around Marisa and gave her the support that they knew she needed. Everyone's first day back had been difficult, but they knew Marisa had suffered more than any of them. She had been closest to Bethany and had the rockiest recovery. To make matters worse, she wasn't able to attend Bethany's funeral to get the closure she needed.

"It's time to start healing," she told her friends. "Bethany's mom said it best, 'she lives on through us.' We have to be strong for Bethany." That had been how their week began. The accident had brought them closer, and they depended on each other for their healing.

Marisa was happy to be back at school, but when Friday arrived, she welcomed the break. She needed the break. It had been a long, emotional week. Because of Thanksgiving, there was no football game to prepare for. That was another blessing.

She got a text from Shane, "Meet at da spot." She knew that meant for her to go to the student parking lot. *She must have driven to school again.* Marisa wasn't ready to be in a car with her friends just yet. She was still having nightmares. In her dreams, Brandi and Shane died, but she lived. No matter how many times she tried to save them, she couldn't. She woke up in a puddle of her own sweat for many nights after the accident. No, she was not planning on getting into a car with Shane behind the wheel. It wasn't worth the risk.

When she got to the parking lot, she

could see Shane and Brandi talking to a group of people. She wasn't in the mood to socialize. She just wanted to go home, eat some popcorn, and retreat under her covers, watching all the soap operas she had missed during the week.

"Hey," she said as she walked up.

"Hey to you," she heard as Trent stepped out from behind his truck.

"Surprise," her two friends said in unison as Ashton rolled down the window on the passenger's side.

"Want your spot, li'l mama?" he asked.

"Nah, I don't have a spot in there. I'm good," she said, uninterested in the surprise her friends had given her.

"It's like that? Can we at least sit down at Jerry's and have a burger or something?"

"Please, Mari. It'll be just like old times," Brandi pleaded with her.

"You know you want to," Shane said, tickling her sides.

"Stop it," she said, fussing at Shane and

trying not to laugh. "Okay, okay. I'll go, but it's for you, not him." She rolled her eyes at Trent and got in the backseat.

"I can hear you," Trent told her.

"And?" she snapped at him. His smile still made her knees weak and her stomach dance, but she didn't want him to know that. They pulled up at Jerry's and went to their usual table.

When the workers at Jerry's saw Trent, it was as if a mega-star had come home. Everything they ordered was comped by the owner. Marisa rolled her eyes while everyone tripped all over themselves to wait on him. "Seriously?" she said out loud.

"You know you missed him. Stop frontin', Mari," Brandi whispered to her friend.

"I did, Bran, but he didn't miss me. Whatever. This is stupid."

"I got you your favorite," he said, sitting down with a basket of chili cheese fries.

"I'm not hungry."

"How long are you going to make me suffer, Mari? I drove all the way down here after your accident, twenty hours on the road, ten here and ten back."

"Boohoo. I didn't ask you to do that."

"Yeah, but I did it because I love you," Trent replied.

"Oh, is that right? Now you love me? Did you tell that female who was answering your phone the same thing?"

There was complete silence at the table. You could have heard a pin drop as Ashton, Brandi, and Shane watched the drama unfold.

"I ... nobody answers my phone."

"Yeah, well, that's a lie. She calls you 'bay,' right? 'Bay, are you still in the shower?' " she said mockingly.

"You don't understand, Mari. I'm not in high school anymore. College is hard. Harder than I thought. I had to find my way."

"You had to find your way? What about me? I was lost too. You left me here in Port

City all alone, then you refused to take my calls." Her voice was loud and shrill.

"You're making a scene, Mari," Shane told her gently, touching her hand.

"I don't care," she snapped at her. "He needs to hear this. I went down a lonely, dark road, and it ended in tragedy. Look at my face! I'm scarred for life and Bethany's dead! I was running from the emptiness that *you* left me with, and now you want to show up here, acting like I'm the bad guy. I am not the bad guy!" She ran from the restaurant, crying. Trent stood up to go after her.

"Don't, okay? Just don't," Shane warned him, following Marisa. He sat back down.

"How could you, Trent?" Brandi asked him as she chased after her two best friends.

Shane hugged Marisa as she cried. "I was too embarrassed to tell you."

"You could have told us. We would have understood."

"You know I would understand. You still did better than me on choosing a boyfriend. Shoot, I have the worst taste in guys," Brandi joked, rubbing her friend's back.

They all laughed. "You really do, Brandi," Marisa said, laughing through her tears.

Trent and Ashton walked out of Jerry's with all the food packed up. "Let me get y'all home," Trent said, never looking them in the eyes. He went his normal route and took everybody home but Marisa. Then he drove to the seawall so that they could be alone. "So this is where it happened, huh?" he asked.

She stared out the window, trying to escape the conversation. "Take me home, Trent." She didn't want to be alone with him. There was too much pain to hash out, and she wasn't up to it. "You'll go back to Arkansas in a week, and I'll still be here. It's time to let go."

"I don't want to let you go."

"You have to. I can't afford to hurt anymore. I don't have the strength."

"Marisa, I'm sorry. I'm truly sorry. There are no good excuses for what I did."

"It's okay, Trent. It's over. I have to move on now. I loved you hard, but now I have to love me."

He left the scene of the accident and drove her home. When they arrived, he got out of the car and opened her door. He extended his hand and helped her out of the truck. When she stood in front of him, he looked down at her. "You'll always be the one, Marisa."

"Good luck, Trent," she said, and kissed him gently on the lips.

He grabbed her and hugged her tight. Tears fell from his eyes as he said good-bye. "Under different circumstances, we would have made it, you know?"

She touched his face gently and walked into her house. Another chapter closed.

CHAPTER 17

Shane

The weeks after Shane and Coach Rob's kiss in the gym had been awkward. They tried to avoid each other as much as they could. They both knew they had played with fire that day, and they had to stop before they wound up getting burned. After avoiding him in the days leading up to the Thanksgiving break, and then not talking to him at all over the break, Shane had to admit it to herself: she missed him.

Shane sat in the girls' gym, trying to think of an excuse to go to Coach's office, but she couldn't come up with anything relevant. She decided to talk to him about the events that had transpired over Thanksgiving break. She wanted his advice about how to help Marisa over her rough patch. She knocked on the door to his office.

"Hey, Coach, you have a minute?"

He looked up at her over the papers he was grading and smiled. "For you? Always."

His words made her blush and awakened her body. She hadn't come here for that. Oh, who was she kidding? Yes, she had.

"I just wanted to talk to you about Thanksgiving break. I needed a little advice."

"I'm all ears," he said, placing the papers he was grading back on his desk.

She detailed the story about Trent and Marisa. She asked him how she could help Marisa through this tough time. He began to give her the advice she wanted, but she wasn't listening, she was watching. She watched as his lips parted to speak. They seemed to be inviting her in for another encounter. "Shane," he said, trying to get her attention back.

"Oh, huh?" she asked, attempting to gather her thoughts and move them in a different direction. She didn't even know why he had called her name.

"Are you okay? I asked you a question."

She swallowed hard, pushing her thoughts away. She couldn't even imagine her dad's reaction if this ever got out. She was putting his job in jeopardy on the town's city council. Everyone knew her dad. What she was feeling was scandalous and wrong. Her secret crush could bring the wrong kind of publicity if it ever became public knowledge. *I know Dad's going to kill me, but I can't seem to make these feelings go away.*

"Are you okay?" he asked again. This time his voice softened. It was as if he figured out she was sitting there for reasons other than the ones she said.

"I'm not okay. I can't stop thinking about you. It's like you're invading my mind or something. I can't take this anymore," she said, moving to the other side of the desk and sitting near him.

"Shane, don't do this," he said breathlessly, standing up next to her. "Don't you know who your father is? Because I do. I'd never work in Port City again. I can't risk it all for—"

She began to kiss him. She could not help herself. He did not resist. "Now this is what I came for," she said.

He pulled away, looking at her suspiciously, but not for long. They kissed again. There was a knock on his office door, startling them.

"Coach Rob?" The door opened just a crack. It was the captain of the volleyball team, Kylie. She also had a major crush on the coach, but she wasn't as discrete about it as Shane was.

Shane rushed to the file cabinet, as though she had been helping with Coach's work. Kylie looked at her through narrowed eyes.

"Coach, I'll finish this tomorrow," Shane said, leaving the office. "Bye, Kylie."

"Uh-huh. Bye, Shane," Kylie said, rolling her eyes.

As soon as Shane walked out of the office, she collapsed against a wall in the gymnasium. *This man has my head all screwed up.* She went to the restroom and splashed cold water on her face. She smiled as she looked at her reflection in the mirror. If she was feeling like this, she knew he was too.

She enjoyed the attention, and even more, she enjoyed driving him crazy. She knew she had the power. And it felt good. She had made an adult go against his better judgment, and she loved it. The fact that he was taboo made him even more appealing. "Sorry, Coach, I just can't help myself," she said to her reflection with a wicked grin.

CHAPTER 18

Brandi

Brandi's sincere determination not to date seemed to waver. As usual. No matter how many promises she made to herself, she made the same mistakes repeatedly. She stared at her herself, disappointed with her choices.

She really wanted to pick up the phone and call Dub. She had been missing him ever since Flo had challenged her and pretty much ended Brandi's relationship with him. She wasn't sure if she would ever get the real story of what happened between them, but she knew Flo and Dub had history. That was definite.

She went downstairs to have breakfast with her family. Her parents and Raven were already at the table.

"Good morning," she said solemnly to her family.

"Good morning," they said, noticing her glum mood. Her mom and dad looked at each other, but neither knew what was bothering their daughter. It was always something when raising a teenager. Brandi was mature, but she was still a teenager.

Her father was the first to reach out. He gently touched Brandi's hand. She was playing with her eggs and not eating them. "You okay?"

Brandi stopped what she was doing, but she didn't answer her father. He motioned to his wife and youngest daughter to leave them alone for a second. He knew something had been bothering Brandi, but he couldn't put his finger on what it was.

"Why are you sad, baby?" he asked his daughter.

"I'm horrible at dating, Dad. I keep picking the wrong guys. I don't think I'm ever going to get this right."

The daddy inside of him wanted to tell her that she was too young to date. He couldn't even imagine anyone putting moves on his sweet baby girl. He had been a boy once. He knew how they thought.

"Well, baby, that's what being a teenager is about. You will make mistakes, but the key is to learn from them. Shoot, I made enough mistakes for the both of us. I think it's part of the reason you don't know a good guy when you see one. Daddy's sorry about that."

"Thanks, Daddy. That means a lot."

"You're a great girl, Brandi. When you find the right guy, it will just click. Always remember that."

"I will, Daddy. Thanks again."

"Now, how's Marisa doing?"

"She's better. I think coming back to school really did help." She thought for a moment. "I think you're right about teenagers making mistakes. Mari had a really good guy, but their relationship still ended badly. Maybe these high school years help us so we don't mess up so bad when we get older. There has to be a learning curve."

She kissed her father and ran up the stairs to get dressed. She was going Christmas shopping with Shane and Marisa. With all the drama in their lives, they were getting a late start this year.

When she came downstairs to let her mother know she was ready, Raven was sitting in the den with her purse on her lap. "You are not leaving me again. I'm sick of y'all having all of the fun without me."

That's the way Brandi's life looked to her little sister, fun and exciting. Raven had no idea how stressful it was navigating through the teen years.

When they arrived at the mall, Shane

and Marisa were already there. They met at the food court to grab some lunch and map out a plan. The goal was to get the things they needed and get out of there as fast as possible. It seemed like everyone was at the mall. The familiar faces kept on popping up at every corner.

"I really hope that Dub isn't here. I do not want to see him."

"Why, B? I love Dub," Raven told her, smiling broadly.

She hadn't told her little sister about their almost relationship or about her run-in with Lil Flo. Raven loved Lil Flo. She downloaded all her music and knew all the words to her songs. Brandi didn't want to alert her sister to the fact that she had an issue with Flo.

Brandi's thoughts seemed to conjure them both up. It was like the universe was playing a sick joke because as she rounded the corner, Flo and Dub were there signing autographs. When Dub saw Brandi, he chased after her, even though she made it obvious she did not want to talk to him.

"B! Two seconds ... just two seconds," Dub pleaded.

"What, Dub?" she asked, turning around, annoyed by his presence. It was as if all the feelings she had for him were gone. Her father's words played in her head. *You're a great girl, Brandi. When you find the right guy, it will just click*

"Hey, Dub!" Raven said, happy that he was talking to them.

"Hey, RaRa," he said, giving her a kiss on the cheek. It made her day. "Bran, I just wanted to apologize. I never meant to hurt you."

"RaRa, give me a minute," Brandi said to her sister, who went to stand with Marisa and Shane. She looked disappointed. Brandi could see Flo eyeing them as she finished up with her fans. But she didn't care any more. She gave Flo a cold stare and turned her attention back to Dub.

"It's over. You have to deal with losing me. I'm a *great* girl, and I would have been good to you. You wanted something else, though. Now go deal with Flo. She's waiting for you. And good luck, *Devin*. I have a feeling you're going to need it. Because she is so sweet and caring. Not! He's all yours, Flo! You can stop eyeballing me now."

Brandi flipped her thick black hair, turned, and swung her hips so he could watch her walk away. She looked back to make sure she had his attention, but she already knew that he was still watching.

"Good job," Shane told her proudly.

"Yeah, now for some me time."

"No, some we time," Raven said, grabbing her sister's hand.

CHAPTER 19

Marisa

There was only one football game left in the regular season, and Marisa had not twirled at all since the accident. When she was approached by her twirling coach to perform a solo at the last game, she was shocked. In her mind, she wouldn't twirl again until her senior year, yet here she was in the backyard trying to perfect a three-baton routine. She became frustrated when she couldn't nail a spin that had once been easy. She threw her batons on the ground. She wished she had never agreed to perform at the game.

"It can't be that bad."

She turned quickly to see who had invaded her private practice time. It was her modeling agent, Marcie Miller.

"Marcie? Hey, I'm sorry that I haven't—"

"Returned any of my calls?"

"Yeah, that," she responded sheepishly. Marisa quickly turned away when she realized that Marcie was studying her face. Tears welled up in her eyes. She didn't want Marcie to see her cry.

"Marisa?" Marcie asked, stepping around to face her.

"I don't want you to look at me. I know I've let you down."

"Is that what you are worried about? Letting me down? Are you serious?" Marcie laughed a bit at the absurdity of the statement. "Darling, I can't imagine living through what you lived through. If it had been me at that point in my modeling career, I would have been devastated too. That's why I'm here. To help you."

"You don't have to do that, Marcie. I know that you don't want to represent me anymore. It's okay."

"Oh, Marisa. That's not how this works. I'm not abandoning you because you were in an accident."

"You're not?" She looked up at Marcie's face for the first time. There was a huge grin there.

"No, you have an appointment over Christmas break to see the best plastic surgeon in Beverly Hills. I'm not losing my best model over a few scars."

"Oh my God, Marcie. Are you serious?" Marisa paused, thinking about what Marcie had just proposed. "My family can't afford that. I can't afford that."

"Our agency has already worked something out with the doctor. He heard your story and very much wanted to help you. We need to do a 'before' and 'after' shoot for his office. You will be the face of Sculptique of Beverly Hills. Will that be okay with you? Are you up to this? I know you've gone through a lot."

"I'm more than okay with it, Marcie. Thank you so much. I don't know how I will ever repay you. You have changed my life." She hugged her agent tightly. She knew her emotional behavior wasn't professional, but she couldn't help it. More tears fell. She laughed through them as she pulled away. "I thought you came here to fire me. Guess I should have answered your calls a long time ago, huh?"

"Next time, pick up the phone. Then I don't have to drive all the way to Port City and hunt you down. Now take me for some of those barbequed crabs y'all are famous for."

They went to a restaurant and hurt themselves as they stuffed their bodies full of barbeque. By the time Marcie dropped Marisa back home, it was dark. There was no more time to practice her routine. She promised herself she would work on it until it was flawless. After all, she had a new lease on life.

Marisa wasn't ready to share her good news or her new attitude. Not just yet. She was still reeling from knowing she would not lose her modeling career. It made her believe that anything was possible.

As she spun around on the football field Friday night, all of Port City was there. When she picked up her last baton, the crowd went wild. Marisa unfurled a large picture of Bethany that she had made into a flag. She ran around the twirlers, waving the flag on the end of her baton. Then the other twirlers joined her and picked up their special batons adorned with Bethany's face. From the stands, they could hear students shouting, "We love you, Bethany." When their routine was over, there wasn't a dry eye in the stands. It was their moment to heal, to grieve, and to remember. Finally, closure didn't feel so far away.

THE ACCIDENT

Epilogue

$\mathcal{G}$oing into the Christmas break, Brandi, Shane, and Marisa knew that it would be hard to schedule time with each other. The holidays were always crazy. They decided to plan a girls' day to unwind and review their lives over the past year. Their first stop was the Nail Emporium, which had the best technicians in Port City.

"Three mani-pedis!" the owner shouted once they told her what they needed. They enjoyed the fact that each of them could go to a different nail tech and still come out flawless. Most other salons had one girl who could work magic. But here they were all truly talented. It didn't hurt that the techs gave a great foot massage too.

They settled into their massage chairs and relaxed. "I could get used to this. I love the holidays," Shane said, leaning back with her eyes closed. "No school, no homework, no worries."

Marisa sat in the seat next to Shane, flipping through her favorite magazine. "I need an outfit for the Christmas party my family is going to this year. Can we go shopping when we leave here?"

"Yes, yes, and yes," Brandi responded. "I need to get a gift for my mom from Raven and me. I've purchased my dad's gift already. Shoot, we need to eat first. I'm starving."

"I already decided I want to go to the Cheesecake Factory," Shane announced, opening her eyes.

"Yum, yum, and yum," Brandi said. "I'll cosign to going to Cheesecake."

"Stop saying everything in threes, 'k?" Shane said, narrowing her eyes at Brandi, who made a face back at her.

"I'm getting a salad no matter where we go. No holiday indulgence for me," Marisa informed them.

"What? Why? I thought you were taking a break from modeling," Brandi said, giving Shane a confused look. They both knew Marisa wasn't going to be able to model for a while. The last thing they wanted was to give her a reality check.

"Nope. I have some news," Marisa sang to her friends, her face lighting up like a Christmas tree.

"Do tell," Shane said, matching her excitement as she peeked around Brandi to get a better look at Marisa.

Marisa had kept her meeting with Marcie Miller quiet until now. She outlined everything Marcie had told her about the surgery that would make her scars invisible. She told them about the offer from

Sculptique of Beverly Hills and about the trip she was scheduled to take after Christmas.

Brandi and Shane were as excited as Marisa. They knew this offer was just as life-changing as her first modeling job with Gap.

Marisa had traveled a long road. They had done all they could to help her through the heartache, but they didn't have the power to fix all her wounds. Marcie Miller had come into her life just in time to make a real difference. They completed their mani-pedi session and sat under the nail dryer, waiting for their hands and feet to finish.

"Girl, we are so happy for you," Brandi told Marisa.

As soon as their nails were dry, they went to the Cheesecake Factory, which was connected to the mall. "Well, we are *so* celebrating," Shane said, lifting her Shirley Temple to meet her friends' glasses. "To

Marisa, for having the courage to get back up and be all that she can be."

"I'll drink to that!" Brandi said.

Their food arrived and they dove in: fried macaroni and cheese, tuna tartar, mini-crab cakes, and salad. They barely spoke as they ate, giving Shane a lot of time to think. Maybe too much time. During their silence, she blurted out, "I have a confession!"

Both Brandi and Marisa dropped their forks and looked at their friend. Shane's confessions were never, "Oh, I ate a piece of chocolate cake," or "I borrowed your belt and ruined it." Those were simple things. Those could be fixed. Shane's were usually much more complicated. And dramatic.

"Spill it," Brandi said, studying her friend's mischievous smile.

"I kissed Coach Rob." She let her confession dangle in the air and took a bite of her food.

"No," Marisa gasped with her mouth

wide open. Shane nodded her head as Marisa shook hers.

"Who else did you tell?" Brandi asked her in disbelief.

"Seriously? Is that a real question? Nobody. Who else would I tell?"

"This one takes the cake, even for you," Marisa said, looking nervous. She leaned in and whispered, "Did he kiss you back?" Marisa covered her mouth as if it hurt her to ask.

"*Did he?*" Shane mimicked, her eyes filled with longing. "Uh-huh."

Brandi shook her head. "Girl, you are bad. You need to quit."

"She's not bad, just misguided at times," Marisa said, hating the thought of anyone calling her friend bad, even Brandi.

Shane laughed at her friends. They were both right. She could be bad and misguided at times, but she embraced her flaws. She knew her chapter with Coach

Rob wasn't over. No way. And she wanted to explore more.

"You do know you can't see him anymore, right?" Marisa asked her.

"He's my volleyball coach. How am I not going to see him?"

"No! You can see him, you just can't *see* him. You know what she meant, heifer," Brandi said, scolding her friend's bad choices.

"Whatever," Shane said. She changed the subject, as if making out with a teacher was just one small lunch topic. She turned her attention to Brandi. "I'm just happy that *you're* done dating," she told Brandi. "I can't take any more."

"This is not about me. But for real, it's going to take a miracle for *anybody* to holler at me now. I'm tired."

"Girl, you make me tired too. I love Dub, but everything was way cooler when y'all were just friends."

"It's okay to be tired," Marisa told them, looking very serious. "I got tired this year too. It's been hard, especially since losing Bethany. I'm a work in progress right now."

They both reached out to touch their friend's hand. Marisa had been through it. She sat scarred and battered. Her face was still marked with the evidence of an accident. But now she had hope.

It wasn't just about her looks. She had faced herself in the mirror. If she told herself the truth, she could live with the scars. But once she had forgiven herself for Bethany's death, her life started to get better. Things started to turn around for her. Her friends would not let her forget that she was not just her face. She was as beautiful on the inside as she was on the outside.

ABOUT THE AUTHOR

Shannon Freeman

*B*orn and raised in Port Arthur, Texas, Shannon Freeman works full time as an English teacher in her hometown. After completing college at Oral Roberts University, Freeman began her work in the classroom teaching English and oral communications. At that time, the characters of her breakout series, Port City High, began to form, but these characters would not come to life for years. An apartment fire destroyed almost all of the young teacher's worldly possessions before she could begin writing. With nothing to lose, Freeman packed up and headed to Los Angeles, California, to pursue a passion that burned within her since her youth, the entertainment industry.

Beginning in 2001, Freeman made numerous television appearances and enjoyed a rich life full of friends and hard work. In 2008, her world once again changed when she and her husband, Derrick Freeman, found out that they were expecting their first child. Freeman then made the difficult decision to return to Port Arthur and start the family that she had always wanted.

At that time, Freeman returned to the classroom, but entertaining others was still a desire that could not be quenched. Being in the classroom again inspired her to tell the story of Marisa, Shane, and

Brandi that had been evolving for almost a decade. She began to write and the Port City High series was born.

Port City High is the culmination of Freeman's life experiences, including her travels across the United States and Europe. Her stories reflect the friendships she's made across the globe. Port City High is the next breakout series for today's young adult readers. Freeman says, "The topics are relevant and life changing. I just hope that people are touched by my characters' stories as much as I am."